Trappi

Mark Noble Space

Tony Har...

Reader Club

Sign up for Tony's no-spam Reader Club newsletter for a free ebook, exclusive content, and special offers.

Details can be found at the end of TRAPPIST-1.

Copyright Page

Very special thanks to: Robert Brinkman, Wendy Harmsworth, Dean Howard, NASA.gov, Melanie Underwood

Also, thanks to these VIP Beta Reader Club Members: Annette Burgess, Anne Graham, David Green, Jim Hewlett, Greg Hills, Scott Kreisler, James McCarthy, Colin Pain, Joe Pedreiro, Mike Ramay, Nigama Ranganatha, Nev Rawlins, Linda Reed, Nigel Revill and Patrick Stakem, who have contributed so much help in raising the quality of my story.

ISBN: 9798645300265
Copyright © Tony Harmsworth 2020
Cover design by Margaret Rainey © 2020
Illustrations by Dan Sutherland © 2020
Illustration adaption Tony Harmsworth © 2020
Published by:
Harmsworth.net
Drumnadrochit
Inverness-shire
IV63 6XJ

i) Story So Far

(Contains spoilers if you haven't read Moonscape)

Note for non-British readers – Tony writes using UK English spelling, punctuation and grammar, plus some US English words where appropriate as there are various nationalities within these stories. Miles and kilometres will both be used in the story and, occasionally, inches when appropriate to the storyline.

*It is **strongly** recommended that you read Moonscape **and** Moonstruck before starting this sequel. Thank you.*

Tony Harmsworth

Astronauts Mark Noble and Roy Williams were surveying a moon crater a few miles east of Moonbase in early 2028. A hollow, full of moon dust (regolith), causes Williams, who is driving the moon buggy, to get stuck. A hazardous situation is created because Mark is on the surface, running out of air and the hatch of the buggy is buried in the dust.

In the nick of time, a second buggy arrives to tow the disabled vehicle out of the dust. However, the accident disturbed a tiny hibernating creature, about the size of a ten-year-old child's finger, which attaches itself to the buggy wheel and is transported back to Moonbase.

Inside the garage dome, the entity infects Williams and paralyses his central nervous system. The other astronauts believe that he has died.

The entity learns how to control Williams' body and escapes Moonbase in a buggy. However, the buggy is easily tracked and soon found by other members of the Moonbase crew. Williams is brought back and, although acting a little strangely, he appears to be recovering. The entity has now gained a better understanding of what humans are, and is learning how to hide the fact that it has possessed and is in total control of its victim.

The entity divides and takes over the doctor. Soon, all of the Moonbase crew are possessed except for Mark and his partner, Linda Fuller. Realising they are in existential jeopardy, and after a violent struggle, they escape Moonbase and manage to launch the Dragonstar lander, escaping capture by the possessed humans by a matter of seconds.

After leaving the Lunar Gateway, they head to Earth in their Orion craft. En route, a specimen, sealed in an airtight container, manages to escape and infect Mark.

Because the entities can divide every two days, Mark and Linda realise that the creatures must not be allowed to reach Earth. No one had expected it to be able to escape from a hermetically sealed cylinder, but it had. Its ability to shrink itself to pass through tiny spaces was the cause.

Once Linda realises that Mark is infected, she knows that the only option is to make their Orion to burn up on re-entry to kill both them and the entity, but their capsule had begun its automatic sequence and could not be aborted.

By chance, the outer Van Allen radiation belts, which encircle the Earth, had weakened the entity and the inner Van Allen radiation belts killed it, preventing a global infection. Extraordinary quarantine precautions were still taken by NASA when the Orion was plucked from the sea. The Moonscape story ends after the dead entity was removed from Mark's skull, paving the way for the second book, Moonstruck.

[Seriously, reading beyond here will totally spoil Moonstruck, the second book in the series. There were several twists in the storyline. You have been warned.]

NASA, together with the Chinese who had abandoned their own moonbase, and the Russians who shared both lunar habitats, decide that they must recapture Moonbase from the six possessed humans who were left in occupation. Mark is to lead the mission. Linda, now married to Mark, has been grounded as she is expecting a child.

A force of twenty-eight astronauts, including fourteen military, head for the moon in seven ships, transferring into six Dragonstars at the Lunar Gateway for the mass descent to the surface.

They arrive with bespoke radiation projectors which have been designed to emit similar radiation to that found in the inner Van Allen radiation belts. The projectors should be able to kill the entities. A medical team is travelling with them to be able to extract dead entities from the infected individuals.

When they arrive on the moon, they discover that Moonbase is deserted. Enough spare parts had been taken by the infected astronauts to build a second habitat. Included within the missing spares were particle detectors. They had also dismantled several cosmic ray detectors from Moonbase. No one had any idea why.

During the first sleep period after the force arrive, the possessed are able to gain access to Moonbase and infect almost everyone, only just being stopped at the last minute by Marine Colonel Doug Baker and Mark himself. The military manage to regain control and kill the entities. Using keyhole surgery, the surgeon and his medical team extract the dead parasites. Most people show few side effects and recover quickly.

One of the infected Marines was imprisoned, so that Mark could interrogate her. They were hoping to extract some information from her about what the possessed were doing at the habitat they had constructed in a cave system known as Asimov Rille, eight miles from Moonbase.

Mark discovered that the Marine's entity was able to release the possessed person's mind so that she could speak freely. Communication began and it began to seem that the entities were able to be symbiotic rather than parasitic. The captured one said that was how they were now working with their hosts who were no longer controlled at all.

Mark headed an expedition to the Asimov Rille and contact was made with the possessed. They refused to allow Mark's team into their habitat, because they were justifiably afraid of the projectors. All of the entities in the Rille could have been killed at a stroke. However, a couple of the possessed astronauts, including Roy Williams, agreed to come to a meeting at Moonbase.

During an extremely secure Moonbase meeting, new revelations came to the fore. It seemed that the entities actually enhanced the humans, giving them total recall and improving their mathematical and intellectual abilities.

Mark and his two closest advisers, Anna Stanbury and Bill Wright, came to realise that the entities could actually be a great force for good. During their isolation on the moon, the 'enhanced' humans had managed to push forward scientific boundaries. They had come up with the unification theory of quantum physics with relativity and it looked as if they might have found a way to warp space to permit travel to other star systems.

Mark, Anna and Bill became increasingly worried that the military were influencing NASA and might make a pre-emptive strike on the Asimov Rille to destroy all the entities.

On the advice of Roy Williams, Mark, Anna and Bill took entities from the possessed as an experiment. They were amazed at how brilliant the symbiosis was. It even cured illnesses, cancers and extended human longevity. The military were unaware of the three having been enhanced – the word the possessed preferred to possession or infection.

In the meantime, Colonel Baker and the military had been ordered by generals who were controlling and overruling mission control to attack the Asimov Rille. The possessed surrendered and were brought back to Moonbase where they were irradiated by the military to kill their entities.

However, unknown to the military, Tosh (Dr John MacIntosh), one of the possessed, had come up with a chemical which could be injected into the entities to protect them from the radiation projectors and the Van Allen belts.

When the military irradiated the five possessed humans in the garage dome, they all fell to the floor feigning unconsciousness. The military assumed the entities had been killed, so permitted the medical team to retrieve the unconscious humans for surgery.

The medical team, however, had already become enhanced via Mark, Bill and Anna. Within a few hours, the enhanced people outnumbered the ordinary humans and, in short order, everyone in Moonbase was enhanced.

Mark, with Colonel Baker, then began a subterfuge with NASA, pretending the entities had been exterminated. Mark expressed his fury with NASA and the military in Houston for seeking to destroy all the entities against his advice. NASA and the military did not know, of course, that everyone at Moonbase was now enhanced.

Mark and his team returned to Earth and began to infect the world with the entities.

What follows is an abridged last chapter of Moonstruck to help you get up to speed.

ii) Return to Earth (Abridged from the last chapter of Moonstruck)

Six of us stood by Dragonstar 3 – Anna, Bill, Doug, Tosh, Mary and me. We'd filled the storage section with items which needed returning home and now took our last look around the surface of the moon.

Once sealed in, my enhanced memory took over and I anticipated all of the communications between Anna, the pilot, and the Lunar Gateway.

'Ignition, one, zero!' said the computer.

The Dragonstar lifted off far faster than one would normally expect. The moon's weak gravity was a major factor in the speed of the ascent. Thirty minutes later, we were alongside the Gateway and were soon docked and pulling ourselves through the tunnel in the top of the Dragonstar vehicle into the Gateway. My entity briefly flashed a memory of the fun I'd had in this space with Linda. In my mind I told him to shut up and we began the preparation of an Orion to take us home.

Although Orions were more comfortable with four or five astronauts, we wanted to return together. It would be a squeeze for six, but we were prepared for a few days' discomfort and six rather than four would make our plan easier to complete.

Anna spoke to NASA, agreed our separation time and a steady application of thrust saw us en route to the blue marble we could often see through the porthole. My entity kept directing my gaze towards it. He was even more excited than I.

The moon drifted away from us, or so it seemed, as the journey to Earth began. In three days, we'd be floating in the Pacific off San Diego and the Navy would be lifting us out of the water. Ocean swell was far more nauseating than freefall. Our only fear was that the military on Earth might have developed an even more deadly radiation projector and our entities could be at risk.

After re-entry, the capsule bobbed sickeningly, we all looked at each other and confirmed that Tosh's "vaccination" had worked its wonders. All our entities had survived the journey through the Van Allen belts with only minor ill effects.

We were not allowed to open our capsule and were compelled to wait until the crane on the support ship could lift us out and onto the warship deck where it was immediately irradiated and washed with disinfectant.

Once we emerged, we too were irradiated, as were the interior and storage areas of the capsule. No chances were being taken. My entity did not feel so bad this time. Tosh had told us resistance to radiation would improve.

When I was alone with Bill, I said, 'That was worrying.'

'Yes, they might have found some stronger radiation,' he said.

'Fortunately not,' I replied.

The captain invited us to dinner in his cabin with the first officer. By the time we left, two extremely senior naval officers were enjoying their entities' benefits. I retained my own divided entity for an even more special connection ashore. Tosh had a flask containing at least another thirty entities with which he intended to enhance key individuals at NASA.

The following day, on the quay, I could see Linda. I couldn't wait to hold her in my arms. My entity was eager to explore her condition. He wanted to see whether he could interact with a child in the womb. I expressed concern that he should be careful not to harm either of them and he assured me he'd take extreme care. I knew he would.

Linda and I hugged and were soon back in the hotel. Our first private kiss gave her more than just a loving feeling. I held her tight, steadying her as my entity's twin entered her and introduced herself.

She immediately checked Linda's health and that of the embryo and told us all was right with the world.

∞ ∞ ∞ ∞ ∞ ∞ ∞ ∞ ∞ ∞ ∞

Four weeks later, the number of augmented humans had grown into the hundreds of thousands. In three months, almost everyone on Earth would belong to the new breed of humankind.

The world would change and adapt. I was hoping our exploration of the universe would become a greater priority, and disease, poverty and conflict would become part of history.

Enhanced humankind was facing a new future and I wanted to be part of it.

Linda's bump was beginning to show and already had its own entity. Our little family was benefiting enormously from their having become part of us, and no, we didn't need to evict them to the dressing table when we made love. They enhanced everything!

I received a call from Neil Weston at NASA, who I'd personally augmented during my "resignation meeting" the first week back. 'Mark, is a month's vacation a long enough break?'

'Why? What do you have in mind?' I asked.

'How would you like an interstellar space jaunt?'

'Mary's cracked the problems then?'

'She has,' he said.

'What's the mission?'

'There'll be a test mission first, then on to Trappist-1. You up for it?' he asked.

The phone was on hands-free. I looked at Linda and she nodded.

'Count me in,' I said.

'Better come in tomorrow then. You'll want to assist with the design and picking your crew.'

1 Brave New World

My first duty, when I returned to Earth from the moon, was to report to Neil, the Moonstruck mission director. A sandy-haired New Yorker, Neil was forty-something and balding. He'd once been a good college football player, so had broad shoulders and one of those muscular necks which seemed overly wide. He was clean-shaven and had the pale freckly skin of many redheads.

I entered his office. He looked up from his desk and smiled.

He was aware of my anger with NASA for having allowed the military to destroy the entities in Moonbase. What he had not known, of course, was that we had arranged for all of the astronauts to adopt entities. I had needed to get back to Earth quickly to ensure they spread beyond any chance of quarantine being applied. My excuse for an early return was telling him that I was resigning.

'Lovely to see you, Mark,' he said, walking around his desk and giving me a man hug. He was a friend as much as my boss. 'You're not serious about resigning?'

'Neil, do you realise what destroying the entities did to the advancement of humankind?' I said, continuing the pretence that the entities had all been exterminated.

'We had no choice. The military were certain that to allow any of them to survive could have meant the end of homo sapiens. I'm sorry, but there was no alternative.'

I seated myself in one of his visitor's chairs. 'There *was* a choice,' I told him. 'We could *easily* have set up one of the domes as a study centre. Scientists could have observed and questioned the subjects and learned a huge amount. It was a perfect opportunity. What better place than the moon to study something which we were worried could be infectious. The military denied the world that opportunity. What did the universities tell you? You never said.'

'Both universities were very upset that we had not kept any infected humans. They said the physics was groundbreaking and would have liked to have discussed the science with them,' said Neil. 'But it was out of our hands.'

'Are you sorry?'

He looked at me, removed his spectacles, and laid them on his desk. 'Mark, you know I can't provide a public point of view on this. Surely you've known me long enough to know how I feel about it. We are all pawns in the grand scheme of things.'

I said, 'We've known each other since I joined the astronaut programme. If you want to retain my trust in NASA, I need to know your personal position on this. I need to know just from a friendship point of view. The last few years we've been friends, too. It's important. You can't hide behind the NASA façade.'

He stared blankly at me, then wiped his glasses with a tissue and slotted them back upon his nose. 'Of course I'm sorry, Mark. Of course NASA didn't want to throw away the opportunities which were in that report to the universities. Between you and me, I consider it was a horrendous decision. Bob agrees with me, but we were compelled. He and I even got calls from the Vice President.'

'Well, thanks for that anyway,' I said sarcastically. 'It's good to know that the genocide of an entire race of intelligent beings was at least important enough for the *Vice* President to contact you!'

He threw up his arms. 'What's done is done, Mark. But it is no reason to throw away your career. Withdraw your resignation. Please,' he said, leaning forward and clasping his hands before him.

'First, I want to explain what the loss of the entities means to us, in fact to you,' I said.

'Fire away,' he said relaxing back into his seat. 'I'll take my punishment.'

'They could detect and correct illnesses including hypertension, motor neurone disease, multiple sclerosis, and Parkinson's and they could spot cancers when they began to grow and stop the blood flow to them. The cancerous cells die and disappear from the body in just a matter of weeks. As an experiment, I authorised Anna to host an entity and it found and destroyed a potentially fatal cancer growing in her oesophagus.'

'Anna hosted one? You didn't tell us. It really killed her cancer?' Neil asked.

'It really did,' I said. 'Now think on this – because of your decision, all of the millions of cancer deaths in the world are now an unnecessary evil. More than ninety-five per cent could have been stopped. *You* have put a death sentence *on ten million people* who will die of cancer in the next year alone. You have caused millions to live with dementia which could have been prevented before it started and eased for existing cases. The common cold would have been eradicated, and flu and other viruses would vanish. There would never again be a plague like COVID-19. The entities would have been able to marshal the body's defences to find and kill them all.'

He looked at me with sadness in his eyes.

'And it doesn't stop there,' I continued. 'The improvement in intellect would have seen us breaking free from, not only the Earth, but the solar system too. All lost. All sacrificed on the altar of an all-knowing government and its paranoid military.'

He said nothing.

'Do you understand the seriousness and long-term implications of what you have done?'

He took a deep breath and sat more upright in his chair. 'Yes. I do. But NASA's hands were tied. We couldn't stop it. I'm truly sorry.'

We stared at each other. Was the time right or should I save it for another occasion? My entity prodded me to take the opportunity.

'Would you like to help to put it right?' I asked.

'If only, but how? Bob and I tried every type of reasoning with General Gilby. He just wouldn't listen.'

'Watch!' I said and removed a ballpoint pen from my pocket.

I stood it on my finger and, with almost invisible adjustments, it stayed vertical. Neil looked at the pen with a puzzled gaze.

'Try it,' I said, reaching over the desk to give him the pen.

He placed it on his finger and within a second or two it had tumbled onto the inlaid leather. He tried again with worse results. 'What's the trick?'

'Give it back,' I said.

I took the pen, balanced it on my left index finger, tossed it to my right hand and then grabbed more from his desk tidy, which was full of pens and pencils. I put a second pen on my left hand, then more on both hands.

Neil laughed, 'Come on, Mark. What's the trick?'

'Patience,' I said, replacing my own pen in my jacket pocket and returning his to the desk tidy. I handed him a small notepad. 'Write down two seven figure numbers under each other.'

Again he looked at me in a puzzled manner, scribbled some digits and passed it back to me.

I looked at the two numbers, 7,322,809 and 3,457,336 for a few seconds then wrote 25,317,411,176,824 beneath them and passed it back. 'Check the multiplication,' I challenged.

He carefully copied the numbers into his laptop, multiplied them and then expanded the e-number into digits which matched mine exactly.

He looked hard at me. 'That is *not* possible,' he stated.

'Neil, it *is* possible. I just did it!' I said.

'How? Stop messing about, Mark. What's going on?'

'Can't you guess?' I said, sitting back in my chair.

I watched his face change from puzzlement to realisation. 'You aren't?'

'Aren't what?'

'Infected.'

'No, I'm not *infected*, I'm *enhanced*,' I said.

He sat silently, staring at me. I guessed options were going through his mind, from calling for help, to running away.

More than two minutes passed. A long time to sit in silence looking at someone who might be a deadly enemy but had always been a colleague and friend.

'How?'

'We experimented on Moonbase. What I said about Anna's cancer was true. We discovered that it was a pure symbiosis, not an infection. We knew we had to stop the military and took steps to enhance everyone including the military members of the crew. Tosh had discovered a way to protect the entities from the radiation used by the projectors and also that of the Van Allen belts. We were safe to return home.'

'But you could infect me?' he said, his voice trembling.

'No, but I could *enhance* you.'

'Are you really Mark? How do I know?'

'Ask me anything.'

'You really have one of these things inside you?' he asked, incredulous.

'I do.'

'And there's no compulsion to infect me?'

'Not a compulsion, but I think you would appreciate one. Now that enhanced humans are increasing in number, no unenhanced person would be of any use to the future space programme. You can see what a difference it has made to my physical and intellectual capabilities,' I said.

Again he sat in silence, considering what I'd said.

'You have one with you?' he asked.

I removed a small metal container from my side pocket and passed it to him. 'This is the most wonderful gift you will ever receive. You said you'd like to put things right. Here is the opportunity. Prove it!'

He turned the box over in his hand. The top showed the stars and stripes. He read the side, 'Singer Accessories! You want me to take up sewing?' He smiled.

'Just a convenient box which Linda had.'

'What if I change my mind?' he asked.

'Ask him to leave you.'

'You're joking. All that trouble with you and Linda escaping Moonbase and all that was needed was for you to ask them to get out of your heads?'

I placed my hand on the walnut edge of his desk. My entity, almost clear and slightly glistening, emerged from the back of my hand and moved onto the desk. 'That's mine,' I said. 'When they first took over Roy and the others, they were in a battle for supremacy. They believed that if they had released free will back to any of the humans at the time, they'd have cried "invasion". It meant there was never an attempt at symbiosis in those early days. It was always about outright control. Remember, that entire first event only lasted a few days. After Linda and I escaped, they were isolated at Moonbase and able to begin to really work together. Very quickly, they realised that symbiosis was the only way forward with such a powerful species as us. What began as absolute control, soon developed into symbiosis as both entity and host worked together.'

I turned my hand sideways and my entity returned home.

'I'm not sure I'd like one of these things forever talking to me in my head. I like my life and my thoughts to be mine.'

'Neil, I would not offer you something which would harm you. I promise,' I said. 'Normally, they sit in the background helping you to understand things more clearly, improving your ability to explain things and operate things. He doesn't sit in my head saying, "do that this way", "it would be better if you said it this way", or telling me off for doing things in a different way to what it thinks is best.'

He opened the box and looked inside.

'Your intellect is improved, your thinking sharper and more specific, your dexterity, like that pen trick, is not him controlling my hands, but him having given me the ability to control my motor systems far more effectively,' I said.

His gaze returned to the contents of the box. 'There's two of them,' he said.

'One for Miriam.'

'What do I do?'

'Sit back in your chair and offer the back of your hand. You will feel odd for a while and he will probably explore some of your memories. If you want him to stop, just think the instruction. I'm here to help you, but you'll soon find that you'll get all the help you need from the entity.'

He was still hesitant. We sat quietly. There was no point in trying to force the issue. Eventually he overcame his natural reluctance, relaxed, and offered his hand.

2 Resistance

During the early weeks after my return from the moon, more of the expeditionary force also returned to their homes in the USA, China, Europe, Britain, India and Russia. The enhancement of humankind was now unstoppable.

The enhanced humans' policy was to first enhance people who were close to us as friends or relations. This stopped the bulk of resistance, but not all and there were always those who saw it as an infringement to their liberties, even if it was saving and extending their lives.

Lockheed were one of the main manufacturing and component suppliers for the Orion spacecraft after the original Artemis programme. One of their senior managers, Susan Holby, did cause a problem. After being enhanced, she decided to blow the whistle, and having extensive media contacts her outcry went worldwide.

We knew it was all way too late to stop the spread of the entities, so we didn't react at all, but it did cause some trouble.

All of a sudden, there were news and current affairs programmes asking the question. Did the Lunar Regolith Parasites (LRPs) manage to get to Earth? Are they taking us over by stealth? Did they survive the lunar eradication?

All entities knew that force should never be used with humans after the first few hours while they were learning the benefits of enhancement. Susan's entity was shocked by her severe adverse reaction and had trouble knowing how to deal with the situation. She went to great lengths to show Susan how lives were being saved, chronic diseases being conquered, life extended and so on. Her entity even found an early cancer in Susan which she insisted be checked via an MRI scan to prove it was real. It still didn't convince Susan that the enhancement was beneficial, even after showing her that the cancer had later disappeared. She continued to make as much noise as possible about being taken over by an LRP.

The general public became bored with her tirades, but it enthralled unenhanced journalists who were not convinced about the truth of Susan's story at first, but gradually became more suspicious. Their natural reaction was to approach the Moonstruck expeditionary members for comment. Naturally, I was a prime target as the leader of the expedition and continuing to work with NASA.

When the inevitable interview was requested, I restricted it to seven journalists, and we all sat in a small lounge area at the Johnson Space Center.

'Dr Noble, you'll know of the claim that parasites were brought back from the moon and are gradually taking over the general public,' said the New York Times leader writer.

'And your question is?' I asked.

'Well, did you bring the parasites back? Are you part of the invasion.'

'You need to understand the context of what happened on the moon from January through to the end of April,' I said.

'Did you bring parasites back?' prompted another journalist. They were determined not to be fobbed off.

'In order for me to answer that, you need to allow me to set the context. If you will not allow that then this interview is over,' I said, then sat silently.

After a few tens of seconds of uncomfortable silence, the NYT journalist said, 'Okay. What do you want to say?'

'I just want to set the context,' I said, sipping my water, my entity informing me of the mood of my audience and helping me keep calm and measured in the telling. 'The first encounter was sheer chance. One of the entities which had become our hippocampi millions of years ago, had never made it to Earth. It was stuck in deep moon dust until the buggy used by Dr Williams and myself fell into a dust pit near the crater designated as Timocharis Delta.'

'We know all of that,' said another journalist.

I lifted my arms in exasperation. 'If there is somewhere you need to be that is more important than this, please go,' I said and sat in silence pointedly.

When he realised I was not going to say anything further, he apologised and I was able to continue. My entity was actually helping me control the audience. 'The prime objective of these creatures is to join with a living being. They were symbiotes needing to be inside an animal in order to help that animal be more successful. Initially we believed them to be harmful parasites, intent on control, but later found that it wasn't the case.

'On our return to Moonbase on that first day, Dr Williams was apparently attacked by the alien entity, which disabled him. It needed to learn about its host and could not do that while a struggle was taking place between itself and its host. It took over Dr Williams' central nervous system so effectively, that he appeared dead, even to the Moonbase medical doctor, Dr MacIntosh.

'The battle between the first entity and Dr Williams became existential and the entity came to believe that it needed to conquer Moonbase before it could travel to Earth. All the time, it was learning about us, realising we were intelligent thinking creatures. It believed that only total control of us would suffice. It didn't dare release its hold on its victim until everyone was infected.

'Within a day or so, it had reproduced and began controlling Dr MacIntosh. The rest of the crew were unaware of this at the time.

'The entities could only reproduce every two days, but by day five, they had already occupied six of the Moonbase crew. Only myself and my wife, Linda, were free.'

'We know all of this,' said the man from Reuters.

'You *might* know *some* of the facts,' I said, 'but you *don't* understand the context. Am I going to be allowed to finish the explanation?'

There were several answers in the affirmative.

'We are now at the point where six of the Moonbase crew were what we called, "infected". Linda and I believed we were in mortal peril and escaped, accidentally killing Blake Smith, the Moonbase commander, as he tried to stop us boarding our Dragonstar.

'One of the entities, as you know, "infected" me as we were re-entering Earth's atmosphere. We were so alarmed by this that Linda tried to destroy the spacecraft, but was too late to do so.

'You need to understand that, at this point in the story, we all felt that we'd encountered a creature which was

28

intent on world domination. There had *never* been such an existential threat to mankind. It was obvious that we needed to return to the moon and destroy them. They were too dangerous to be allowed to survive. There was serious discussion of abandoning the moon completely in case there were more entities hiding in the regolith. The military seriously suggested resolving the Moonbase problem with a nuclear bomb!'

I leaned forward, picked up my glass of water and took another deep draught before continuing. It gave the idea of the nuke time to sink in.

'The bomb idea was kept in the background. When we returned to the moon, some of us soon discovered that the "infected" astronauts had come to believe that it wasn't a harmful parasitic infection, but a beneficial symbiosis. We learned that the entities could exit their hosts and even while still within them, they could refrain from taking any control of the hosts.

'Meetings followed with the people hosting the entities and we found out that there was absolutely nothing sinister or damaging about the creatures. In fact, the opposite was the case. They could enhance our intellect, cure our diseases and illnesses and extend our longevity.

'To understand their power and their interaction with humans, you need to think about it, not as one having power over the other, but them and us working together to achieve more than we would as individuals. The entities learned, too, that total control, using pain as the instrument to control humans, was never going to produce the desired cooperation and only offered the prospect of eternal conflict.

'Does that make sense?' I asked and saw most of the heads nod.

'By this time, some might say understandably, the paranoid military generals here on Earth had taken over the NASA mission and secret plans were being formulated to wipe the aliens out.

'Despite being the leader of the expeditionary force, I was kept in the dark. This is probably because I was not military. My civilian military adviser, Bill Wright, plus my deputy, Anna Stanbury, were also kept out of the official loop, but, together, we'd independently agreed that we needed to find out exactly what hosting entailed. We considered it worth the risk to our own health.

'The result of our experiment was that, very quickly indeed, we became certain that it was *not* a parasitic invasion, but was a healthy, wonderful symbiosis. The next day the military attacked the entities' habitat at the Asimov Rille, and had orders to capture them all and bring them to Moonbase to be irradiated and have the dead parasites removed.

'Fortunately, no one was aware that Bill, Anna and I were already hosts and we had also enhanced the Moonbase medical team. When the "infected" astronauts from the rille arrived, the military irradiated them, thinking they were killing the entities. What they didn't know was that Dr MacIntosh had developed a protection for the entities. The radiation had almost no effect, but the infected humans all collapsed as if it had. They were stretchered to the surgery, where we plotted together to enhance the military personnel at Moonbase.

'Within twenty-four hours, everyone was enhanced. The military's genocidal action had been foiled and we planned our return to Earth which involved pretending that the entities had all been eradicated.'

'So, you're admitting it?' asked the NYT leader writer with a shocked expression.

'Yes. Watch,' I said and asked my entity to climb out of my hand. 'I am not imprisoned by it. I can be free of it any time I wish.' I noticed that one of the journalists, Rosemary Phelps from CNN, actually stood up and retreated towards the door.

I rotated my hand and my entity was back inside me. I picked up the pen and did the usual pen trick then asked the journalists to give me complex maths tests, which I passed with perfect results.

'Would you like to try one out? As I've shown, they'll leave you if you ask them to,' I said.

They all looked at me sceptically.

'Look. Let me show you,' I said and emptied a box of entities onto a table on my left, a good distance from the journalists. They milled around shining slightly in the light, giving the appearance of slivers of gelatine. Nevertheless, I saw several of the journalists become tense, entering "fight or flight" mode. Rosemary, the retreating woman, took hold of the door handle ready to vamoose.

When nothing happened they calmed down.

'Watch,' I said. I spoke in hushed tones to the entities, then sat back in my chair.

A few seconds later each of them, using their newly found ability to launch themselves several metres, jumped away from the table to the wall on my left. After a few seconds, they returned to the table.

'What the hell?' said one of the journalists who'd leapt to his feet. 'Damn it all, it could have jumped onto me!'

'Yes, but the point is that none of them did. I promise you'll be in full control if you host one. Who wants to try? You can never understand them properly if you are not willing to experience them, and imagine how much better your news story will be with your enhanced intellect and knowledge of exactly what they can do for you.'

'The man from Reuters asked, 'What do I do?'

'You're Art Stelling, yes?' I said, then spoke to the entities, 'One of you – visit Art.'

It jumped from the table to Mr Stelling's neck, he made a small cry and briefly fell back into his seat. Almost instantly he awoke. I could see from his eyes that he was in control. Journalists sitting beside him shuffled away, but I noticed that Rosemary, who'd fled to the door, had released the handle and was now watching intently and scribbling notes.

I knew what was happening inside Mr Stelling's mind. I'd rehearsed it with the entities earlier. It was showing him some total recall from his childhood, youth and adult life. He pulled a pen from his pocket and did some of the pen tricks I'd done earlier.

'How's it feel, Art?' I asked.

'Amazing,' he replied with a silly grin on his face from some past event he was seeing.

'Art, how's your maths?' I asked.

'Hopeless,' he said.

'Tell us pi to ten decimal places,' I said.

He looked at me blankly, then smiled and said, 'Three point one four one five nine two six five three five. Damn it, the thing saw that on a textbook page I was once looking at in my high school maths class!' he said.

'But, with its help, you could have worked it out for yourself if you'd had a mind to,' I said. 'Now ask it to leave you.'

'No. I'd like longer with it,' he said.

'First, *prove* to us that you can make it leave you, Art. The others need to see that it isn't holding you hostage.'

The entity emerged from his neck and jumped back to the table.

'Ooh! That's sore. They hurt when they enter or leave you,' he said.

'It soon goes off. These are not parasites. They are symbiotes,' I said. 'You're all investigative journalists. Shouldn't you be investigating what they can do for you? Help yourselves. Just offer the back of your hands.'

Four came forward, including Art. Experimentation continued and within twenty minutes, all but the CNN woman were enhanced. She said, 'I'm not doing it, but I can meet up with most of you in a week and see how the experiment is going. I'll make myself a personal control.'

'Fine, Rosemary. Sounds like a plan,' I said.

3 Acceptance

Inevitably, the spread of entities tended to grow more quickly in areas where the moon astronauts lived on Earth, although the various NASA, Roscosmos and CSA hubs were also quickly enhanced and through the agencies they reached governments.

Ordinary people's behaviour began to change and the media reported those changes.

The convolutedly named Memorial Hermann Memorial City Medical Center in Houston, had been reporting fewer cases coming to its accident and emergency facility for a week. On the fifteenth of May, with the exception of the passengers from two car crashes and a couple of heart attack victims they had no cases at all and this hit the mainstream news.

When the media began to investigate more thoroughly, it discovered that people were not arriving even for routine tests, chemotherapy, and diabetes clinics. There had been only six more heart attack cases, dialysis patients no longer required treatment and type one diabetes patients found they were producing their own insulin once more.

Naturally, it was linked to the spread of the entities and a change came over people's reactions to the alien visitors. Instead of shying away from enhanced people, an increasing number of the population were actually asking to get one.

Those who rebelled against the aliens fell in number, but there were still small factions who became increasingly violent during the rest of the year. Most faded away when they discovered that enhancement prevented flu, colds, skin conditions, greying hair, and mental illness, as well as improving eyesight, taste, touch, libido, fitness and longevity. The entities, although unable to help people regrow limbs, were still able to help people with physical disabilities, strengthening muscles and limbs through the use of dynamic tension exercises performed by the entities using their host's muscles. They also repaired damaged spinal columns and many paraplegics were soon casting off their wheelchairs and walking normally.

Within three years, all resistance to the aliens had vanished. It is difficult to know whether the entire world had become enhanced, or whether the unenhanced had become like a fringe conspiracy group. Whichever it was, unenhanced humans no longer played any important role.

Complementing the improved health and intellectual abilities of their populations, governments became more compassionate. International borders relaxed and, within five years, most countries had taken the momentous step to gradually abandon the need for the military, other than to swing into action during natural disasters.

All of this happened in parallel to my story today. Now, I'm returning to June 2028 and continuing the story from there.

4 Interstellar Possibilities

First, my return to NASA duties.

Neil's assistant, Brenda, showed me into Neil Weston's office. He stood, as did Mary Carter who had been sitting in a visitor's chair. The forty year old, Mary, had that smooth dark skin which was typical of Pakistani women. Her jet black, shiny hair was wound around her head to keep it under control. I'd seen her release it when we were at Moonbase and it reached beyond her waist.

'Welcome back to work, Mark,' said Neil, shaking my hand and holding my arm to make it more personal. I briefly hugged Mary and we all sat.

Neil's office wasn't grand, but it did have a magnificent view looking across the complex towards Clear Lake. On the walls were many framed photographs of NASA events and people, including one of Neil shaking hands with his namesake, Neil Armstrong, the most famous astronaut who ever lived. Bookcases held reference hardbacks in among files, and copies of biographies of astronauts and engineers.

'So,' said Neil, 'the temptation of an interstellar voyage has piqued your interest?'

'You knew it would. I assume you've cracked the physics, Mary?' I said.

'To some degree,' she replied.

'There is still a lot to do,' said Neil. 'We need a ship, a propulsion method, a crew, test flights and somewhere to go.'

'You said Trappist-1 on the phone,' I said.

'Yes, that seems a good possibility, and I used it as a method to get you to sit up and take note,' said Neil, giving me a "gotcha" smile.

'There are complications,' said Mary. 'The space-folding flight system requires us to be able to zero in on an actual planetary body. If everything works correctly, we will arrive within a hundred thousand miles of the target. As you might imagine, if the target is a planet, we will arrive high above it and will be able to use conventional fuels and propulsion systems to stabilise our speed and get into a lower orbit for a good look at the planet.

'However,' she continued, 'if we make a mistake in targeting and arrive within that sort of distance of the local star instead of one of its planets, it would not be very healthy for us.'

'So, what's happening to improve targeting?' I asked.

'Mary is conducting ongoing work with the ISS,' said Neil.

'Are we trying to do too much?' I asked. 'Why not set our sights on somewhere like Mars. It would also give us some experience landing on a planet. It's one thing getting to Mars, but being able to go from orbit to the surface and back again, is going to require a vehicle and practice. Presumably a Dragonstar could not be adapted for Mars landings?'

'No,' said Neil, 'needs a larger and more powerful vessel.'

'We're not setting off today, then?' I said with a laugh.

'No,' said Mary. 'Much to do. In fact, we're planning a test flight to Mars as part of our preparation for Trappist-1.'

'I called you in,' said Neil, 'to confirm you wanted to command the mission and to hand over the practicalities to you. I'll monitor budgets. I've already transferred a list of manufacturing companies and their chief design contacts to your tablet.'

'I'll need somewhere to work,' I said.

'The military no longer have a liaison officer here, so that office is free. It's two down the corridor from me,' said Neil.

I knew that office. 'General Gilby's old office?' I said, expressing genuine surprise.

'Yes. It's ironic that he vowed you would never work for NASA again, but it is he who has lost his job,' said Neil.

'What's happening with the military? I hear that there are lots of cuts and redundancies.'

'Yes,' confirmed Neil. 'I hear that the armed forces are being cut back to an emergency force which can cope with natural disasters. It's a gradual process, though. At the moment they're concentrating on the decommissioning of nuclear weapons.'

'Surprising that has happened so quickly,' I said.

'Not really. As military leaders became enhanced, they would have quickly enhanced their immediate superiors and juniors. Once a few generals and admirals saw the light, the whole power structure changed... and all that is down to the little friends in our heads

'Thank goodness we stopped the genocide,' I said. They both agreed and I'm sure Mary appreciated that the statement was aimed at Neil.

'Okay, Mark. That's us done,' said Neil. 'Mary wants to take you to her lab. I'm here if you need to talk.' He stood and selected a bunch of folders from the top of one of his filing cabinets. 'You'll need these.' I took them from him. 'They will fill you in on what we've done so far, including suppliers and designers.

∞∞∞∞∞∞∞∞∞∞

Across in another building, Mary's lab was extensive and filled with experimental equipment and laboratory benches. Along one side there were small glazed office cubicles in which a number of people in white coats were working.

'This is the targeting device,' she said, taking me to a bench which had a machine sitting on it. 'Of course for lab testing it has tripod legs, but normally would be built into the bridge of the ship.' She flicked a switch. 'This monitor shows us what it is "seeing".'

The twenty-inch monitor showed the window frame at the far end of the room.

'How does it work?'

Mary pressed some buttons and the image on the screen changed to a red pixelated object, about two inches across. 'This is our best image of the star Trappist-1, taken by a duplicate of this machine on the ISS, but notice this speck here.' She pointed at a tiny grey mark in the blackness.

'Now,' she continued, 'I'm going to zoom in on it.' She pressed a button and I watched the rough red disc

39

grow until most of it was off the screen. The grey spot had increased in size and was now a series of grey squares. It was completely pixelated. 'As you know, Trappist-1 has seven worlds, currently called A to G. The grey spot is one of them. Our problem is that if we target one of those pixels, we could miss the world completely.'

'Which planet is that?' I asked.

Mary looked at a separate tablet. 'It's Trappist-1E, the fifth and one of the most promising worlds. Similar in size to Earth and known to have water vapour in the atmosphere.'

'The candidate we're most likely to select?'

'Yes, although they're all promising.'

'Have you looked at what will be needed to take us there and back? Motors? Fuel? Ship design?' I asked.

'This document explains most of that, including our design considerations,' she said, handing me a thick binder.

'I'm going to have to describe the journey to laypeople and the media. How best can it be explained?'

'That's not easy to answer, Mark. The maths and terminology are extremely complex, even to an enhanced individual.'

'Okay. Try explaining it to me in the simplest possible terms,' I said.

Mary looked at me with the exasperation of someone who knows her subject so well that she cannot possibly understand why anyone else doesn't.

'Right, practical considerations first,' she said in a bored tone of voice. 'Let's take this central pixel as our destination. Using these controls,' she turned dials either side of the screen, 'we bring these crosshairs together over the central pixel.'

I watched her perform the task.

'Now, we introduce the power,' she continued, flicking another switch. 'A directional line is produced leading from the device to the destination. It doesn't exist in our normal universe, but it does exist in the hidden matter, or dark-matter universe. The quantum universe, some are calling it.'

The cross hairs suddenly had a small circle at the very centre. It blinked on and off rapidly. 'Notice that the circle overlaps all of the visible pixels of the planet. This is the problem we have to overcome, that indistinct targeting.'

'Right,' I said, trying to give the impression I understood better than I actually did. My mind might be enhanced but Mary's enhancement moved her further ahead of even the cleverest of us.

'We are now connected with the distant object, although we see nothing in our world. Next we will press a button called "GO" or something equally innocuous. I can't do that here because this is a mock-up.'

'Go?' I said and laughed. She offered a smile, which was as close as you could usually get to a laugh from Mary. Humour seemed to be beneath her in a work environment. 'So, what happens?'

'A great deal more power is applied and the distant object's place in hidden space time is brought to us, but again, nothing is seen. The ship switches its phase to that of hidden matter and becomes invisible here as it moves into what you might call a fifth dimension. Here we would see the ship vanish with a sudden inflow of air. It

41

and its contents would rematerialise in the hidden dark-matter universe. The power is removed and the remote destination is no longer at this end of the targeting line. It snaps back to its original location like a rubber band being released. Our ship is taken with it and will then manoeuvre into orbit around Trappist-1E.'

'What's the power source?' I asked.

'A fusion reactor. We're working on a prototype in the building over there.' She indicated a windowless structure on the far side of the complex.

'How big is it?'

'The reactor? About four metres in diameter, but we'll be able to miniaturise it by at least a factor of four, eventually.'

'And it will fit in the ship?'

'Oh, yes,' she confirmed. 'No problem at all, even the prototype.'

'And we're protected from the radiation, how?'

'A shielded compartment at the back of the ship holds the reactor. Ken will explain.'

'Who's Ken?'

'The chief reactor engineer. I'll send you over to him when we've finished here,' she said, with growing exasperation.

'I still don't understand how the ship gets from A to B,' I said.

She huffed impatiently, then picked up an office stapler. 'Imagine this is the ship. It is sitting in our space time continuum.' She held it out in front of her. 'Its atoms are all behaving perfectly normally and it exists as normal matter. We can see it.' She began to make it tremble. 'Now its atoms are leaving our universe and switching into the hidden universe.

'You can visualise it as turning through ninety degrees, except that the rotation is out of our space time and into another dimension. We call it a fifth dimension, but that is just for convenience.' She turned the stapler and whipped it away with her other hand. 'As it turns, it vanishes. Now it exists in what we might call hyperspace before materialising at its destination by turning through the opposite ninety degrees.' She brought the stapler back to the front of her body. 'And now it is at Trappist-1E,' she said, setting it back down onto the bench.

'I don't understand the physics of it,' I said.

'I wouldn't expect you to.' She pulled a book from a nearby shelf and handed it to me. 'Read this!' she said. 'It'll help.'

The title was *Shortening the Journey,* by Dr Mary Carter. It looked challenging. I placed it with the other folders I was accumulating.

A loud voice came from behind me. 'Well, well. The man who infected the world!'

I turned to see a grinning Tosh marching towards me. A stocky fifty-year-old, his once grey hair had almost returned to its original colour and thickness, thanks to his entity. We hugged. 'Tosh, how are you? Hair looks great. Hope your entity is teaching you to be less argumentative.'

'Ha ha. It's less of a problem now. People just accept that I know best!'

We laughed.

'Do you understand this space-folding system of Mary's?' I asked.

'Of course,' he said and winked.

Mary shrugged and told him to pull the other leg.

We laughed again, and, amazingly, Mary cracked a smile. 'What do you want now, Tosh? I've got a mission commander to educate!'

Tosh ignored her. 'Well, Noble, I wanted to find out who you'd chosen to join me and you on the first mission.'

'Ha,' said Mary and almost did produce a laugh.

'Yes, you're on the shortlist if you want it, Tosh. We need a scientist and medic. As long as you know I'm the boss,' I said.

'Of course you are,' he said and winked at Mary.

'F-off, Tosh. I need my pupil back,' she said.

He slapped my back and left through the door at the end of the laboratory. 'See you later, Tosh,' I shouted after him.

'You understand the basics?' Mary asked.

'Okay. The principle, anyway. I might ask you to run it past me again. What's next?'

'Come through to my office,' she said, and we entered one of the unimpressive glass partitioned rooms. On the bookcase was a model of a Dragonstar and a mock-up of something more akin to the space shuttle.

'Interesting. What is it?' I asked, picking it up, passing it from hand to hand, turning it around and examining it. The model had been 3D printed from some sort of plastic.

'That is what we're considering for a lander,' she said. 'Have you given any thought to how we get down to the surface of the planets we visit, and back up?'

'Only in the most rudimentary way,' I said.

'Anna's working on the exact needs,' said Mary.

'Anna Stanbury?'

'Who else? She's undoubtedly the most experienced NASA pilot. She's not in today, but you'll catch her in the office at the far end of this row of cubicles tomorrow. She's at Boeing today with Chi Wang, examining design proposals.'

'I'll make sure I see her. Chi's involved too?'

'Yes,' she gave a smile. 'And she's got a "thing" going with Tosh.'

'Never!' I said.

'I tell you no lies. Anyway, if you haven't been giving planetfall detailed consideration, let me flag up some problems.'

'Please do.'

She took the shuttle-type lander from me, picked up the Dragonstar from the bookcase, and sat behind her desk with the two models. I sat opposite her.

'Apollo, in the seventies, was the simplest system. A single use spaceship which left half of itself in orbit and half of the remainder on the surface of the moon to save fuel when blasting back to orbit.

'The Artemis landers,' she said, pointing at a rather beautiful photograph of one sitting on the moon, 'used a similar principle and the bottom sections were cannibalised to become part of the first rudimentary habitat prior to the main construction of Moonbase.

'The Dragonstars, as you know, used fuel refined on the moon, and were fuelled up on the surface every couple of trips, so the whole lander blasted back into orbit.' She waved the model Dragonstar around. 'This was ideal as it meant they became the multi-use vehicles we now know and love. Fuel, made from mined water ice on the moon, was virtually free.

'However, since the shuttle programme ended in 2011, we haven't had the capability to soft-land on a planet the size of the Earth. Even worse, we have no way to get a vehicle like the shuttle back into orbit. To do that we would need the planet we are landing on to have an entire space industry capable of strapping a brand new huge fuel tank and two booster rockets to it.' She picked up the shuttle-type model. 'Whichever planet we land on, I can be pretty sure we will not find a sophisticated manufacturing culture to help us take off again.'

'Right. I understand what you're saying. Did you make any progress on the *Star Trek* type beaming device you were looking at?'

'Some, but we've had accidents,' she said hesitantly. I guessed my question had struck a nerve.

'Accidents?'

'We're having great trouble materialising test objects at the required locations. Mostly they arrive too far above the surface and fall up to fifty metres. Not much use to humans, even enhanced humans. More serious was that one test object arrived to one side of its planned location, right into a crane arm. The explosion took out the entire test site and put several people into A&E.'

'ER, you mean?'

'Sorry, my ten years living in Britain coming to the fore,' she said. 'It isn't a good idea for objects to materialise inside other objects. Even the air was a problem, heating to scalding temperatures. If we did "beam" a person to the surface, he or she might not die from the fall, but most certainly would die from first degree burns! The upshot is that we're concentrating on a shuttle-type craft equipped with enough power to get back into orbit. You see how the problems are mounting?'

'Yes,' I said. 'Weight and thrust.'

'Exactly.'

'What about the fusion reactor?'

She looked at me as if I was a child. 'They're fine for generating power, Mark, but not a jot of use at generating the sort of thrust needed to reach escape velocity.'

'Who did you say I need to see in the reactor building?' I asked, thinking it might be best to give Mary some respite from my ignorance.

'Ken Dougal.'

'I'll find my office, drop these folders and pay him a visit. Thanks for the lesson, Mary.'

'Wait,' she said as I stood. 'The team. I'd like to be included too, please, Mark'

'I'll put you on the shortlist with Tosh,' I said.

It seemed that my crew was selecting itself.

∞∞∞∞∞∞∞∞∞∞

The keys to my office were in the door. It faced the same way as Neil's, so had a lovely view towards Clear Lake. Not quite as spacious, but it would do just fine.

47

I locked up and headed over to the reactor building. On the way, I mulled over the crew. Tosh – general science and medic with great experience in orbit and on the moon; Anna – NASA's chief pilot on Orions and Dragonstars; Chi – another extremely skilful pilot with experience on Orions, Dragonstars and Mings; Mary – astrophysicist and expert in the technology the ship would require. Who else?

5 Dinner Guests

Linda, who was now obviously pregnant, entered the dining area carrying a steaming dish of stir-fried chicken, peppers, onions and chillies. I followed her with a terracotta lidded dish of piping hot tortillas.

I topped up the glasses with a wonderfully crisp and fresh Frascati and took my seat.

'Please, dig in,' said Linda, sipping her own lemon and lime concoction.

We all took tortillas and heaped on the stir-fry plus soured cream, guacamole, humous and salsa. Always a messy dinner, especially if you overloaded your tortillas, something I could never resist.

'So,' said Ronnie, her preferred short version of Veronica, 'how's the wee one?' Ronnie was a petite Afro-Caribbean woman of about thirty. Her hair was styled in stunning lemonade braids.

'En tells me the baby is perfectly happy and can't wait to meet the world,' said Linda.

'En?' asked Bill, also Afro-Caribbean, who had once been a professional linebacker and looked it, and ex-army too. Bill Wright was my military consultant and confidant during the Moonstruck expedition.

'Short for entity,' Linda said.

'Does it monitor the baby continually?' asked Ronnie.

'More or less,' said Linda. 'The baby has its own entity and it keeps En in the picture. Must say that it is very reassuring.'

'I'm sure it must be,' said Bill. 'This is delicious.'

I must admit that Linda's weird version of fajitas was the best I'd ever tasted. It was a weekly or bi-weekly treat we could prepare and cook together.

'What have you been up to since we returned from the moon, Bill?' I asked.

'Frankly, nothing much. Even enhanced by my entity, I'm not clever enough to be a NASA technician and the possibility of military work is rapidly disappearing. At the moment I'm helping in the space archive section of the admin building, but, with my entity, we feel it is not making the most of my talents. I might go into personal training, but at forty, I'm not sure how that will be long term.'

'Well,' said Linda, 'you do have the extra longevity with your entity.'

'Yes, and he repaired some old ligament damage in my knee which ended my football career.'

'Right. The health benefits are amazing,' I said. 'I know it's only minor, but I've always had a tendency to hay fever in the past, yet here we are, approaching the peak season and there's no sign of it at all. I'm sure he's at the bottom of it, smothering the allergic reaction.'

'What are you doing at the moment?' asked Ronnie.

'Went back to work on Monday,' I said.

'Where to?' asked Bill.

'Back to NASA,' I said.

'Doing what?' he asked.

'They want me to head a mission to Trappist-1.'

'What's *that* when it's at home?' asked Ronnie, who was a fan of British idioms.

'It's a dwarf red star, about forty light years from here, with a number of interesting exoplanets. Some are believed to have liquid water,' I said.

'Aren't red dwarfs cool stars?' asked Bill.

'Yes. This one is designated ultra-cool. It's about the size of Jupiter but far more massive.'

'If it's cool, why are the planets interesting? Surely they can't harbour life,' said Bill, finishing a tortilla wrap and trying to hide some soured cream which had fallen onto the tablecloth.

Linda said, 'It's half the temperature of the sun. Don't worry about the mess, Bill. This meal is always fraught with spillage.'

'Despite its coolness,' I said, 'what makes it interesting is that it's extremely stable and up to seven billion years old, that's two and a half billion years older than the sun, so life has had much longer to develop,' I said.

'The planets must be far closer to it, then?' said Ronnie.

'Yes,' I said. 'All seven planets orbit Trappist-1 more closely than Mercury orbits the sun.'

'As close as that?' said Ronnie, filling her second wrap.

'Doesn't that mean they must orbit very rapidly?' asked Bill.

'Yes. Amazingly short years,' I said. 'The closest planet orbits once every day and a half and even the seventh has a year of only eighteen days. The orbits and gravitational fields interact and will produce considerable tidal effects, but the system seems incredibly stable.

These planets have been there for much longer than the age of the Earth.'

'And NASA's planning a mission?' said Bill, filling a second wrap. 'You must show me how you make this, Linda. Much better than the supermarket versions.'

'Piece of cake,' said Linda.

I said, 'Mary Carter has almost cracked the physics, the power source is under construction, and the ISS has been practicing the targeting of the space-folding device.'

'Who's going?' asked Ronnie.

'Well, me; Linda's still grounded, so Anna Stanbury and Chi Wang as pilots, Mary Carter wants to go too, Tosh is adamant he's on the crew, and that just leaves me to find one more. Needs to be competent, healthy, one hundred per cent reliable and have astronaut training,' I said.

Out of the corner of my eye, I noticed Bill stop eating and look hard at me. I avoided his gaze and filled my second tortilla, making him wait for eye contact as long as possible. I looked back up and he was still staring at me.

'Yes. You! You great oaf!' I said and laughed.

Bill finished his glass of wine, put it down and looked around at Ronnie.

'Just promise me you'll be careful,' she said, reaching over and squeezing her husband's hand.

'You're serious, Mark?' he asked.

'Sure am. You up for it?'

'Absolutely. Count me in. When do we leave?'

'Ah, we're not quite that ready.' I laughed. 'Come to my office on Monday morning and I'll fill you in. We're probably going to Mars first.'

'Mars! So I might be one of the first people to set foot on Mars?'

'Possibly, but only four of the six of us will land on the surface. Sound interesting?'

'Sounds wonderful! I don't mind watching from orbit.'

After the meal, we played Nutz[1]. A hilarious strategy game which was even faster and more furious now that we all sported our enhancing entities.

---

[1] Nutz – It's a free game designed by the author. Join the free Reader Club to find out how to play it. Details at the end of the book.

6 Florida

Anna held a left bank and the NASA Eclipse 550 jet turned southwards over Titusville towards the main runway of the Space Coast Regional Airport, continuously losing height.

The Indian River Lagoon sparkled in the Florida sunshine and, from the left seat, behind Anna, I could see the Kennedy Space Center in the distance with the Atlantic beyond. We were all qualified pilots, but Anna always took charge when we jetted between the various companies we needed to visit. Today, it was all six of us. Anna, Bill, Chi, Mary, Tosh, and me. I noticed that Tosh and Chi were talking quietly to each other. He'd always been a loner before. Then I saw their fingers intertwining. I pretended not to notice. Tosh was such an uncompromising individual. If he'd finally found a soulmate, that could only be a good thing. Perhaps what Mary had said was true, then.

'Be down in a minute,' Anna said, extending the flaps as we looked straight down the runway. We cleared the last of the buildings and crossed the scrubby woodland on final approach.

Months had passed and we were arriving for a design meeting with Boeing engineers at their Space and Launch Headquarters. One of their buildings was visible to the left of the airport.

The reassuring chirp told us that the wheels were on the ground and the nose swiftly followed. Anna taxied us into the terminal where Boeing had a limo awaiting us.

'Smooth landing,' said Bill.

'Thanks, Bill,' Anna replied as she cut the Pratt and Whitney engines and carried out her post-flight checklist.

Tosh soon had the door open and we waved at Ted Branston, Boeing's chief designer for the still unnamed starship, who had come to meet us personally.

A ten-minute journey saw us arrive at the anonymous, windowless building which housed the prototype. Ted opened the door and we entered a hangar. The starship stood in the centre of it. We all stopped to take photographs.

'Wow!' said Mary. 'Last time I was here, all you had was a polystyrene model and some steel cylinders.'

'Yes,' I agreed. 'It really looks the biz.'

'Well,' said Ted, 'this one really is still just a shell, but all the aerodynamic work has been completed at the Everett factory and we're hoping to begin fitting out soon into the new year. It's a matter of juggling how much we should construct here and how much in Earth orbit. The weight of this beast is well over anything the SLS[2] can handle and JPL[3] are looking at a special one-off launch system. Could need six solid rocket boosters.'

'Wow,' Bill said. 'That's huge.'

'This damn thing called gravity,' Ted said, adding a laugh.

This was the main ship. It would be used to take us to and from our folded-space destinations. It had a certain amount of streamlining to facilitate its initial launch, but once it was in space, it would never touch the ground again.

A skeleton framework in the hangar supported the ship. The main hull consisted of a cylinder forty metres

---

[2] NASA Space Launch System
[3] NASA Jet Propulsion Laboratory

long and four in diameter. At the rear, the fuselage swelled into a sphere which would contain the reactor. It was about seven metres in diameter and looked like the head of a giant microphone. The rear half of the sphere was missing, but we could see it lying over to the right of the hangar.

Ted saw the direction of my gaze. 'We'll be launching the reactor and the bulk of the fittings separately to save weight. It'll be assembled in orbit,' he said.

At the other end of the fuselage was another bulbous feature, not spherical this time but tapered towards the front like a pear drop. This would be the bridge.

'Can we get inside?' asked Chi.

'Come aboard,' said Ted, climbing steps up to the main fuselage. 'Be careful of cables and equipment lying around on the floor. It's a health and safety nightmare at the moment.'

Inside, it really was in a chaotic state, with miles of cables strewn about the cylinder.

'The airlocks will be forward of here,' said Ted. 'This entrance will be sealed. Crew compartments will surround us. Their orientation won't be important as the ship will always be in freefall.'

Tosh walked to the rear. 'Where does this lead? The reactor?' he asked, tapping on a door in a bulbous surface at the rear.

'Yes, it's your access to the reactor and the power generator,' said Ted. 'Of course, there will be at least one other bulkhead between it and the crew to protect from radiation.'

'Why do we need access at all, Ted?' asked Chi. 'Are there any serviceable parts?

'We felt it was important to have access internally,' said Ted. 'It is still under discussion with Ken. We're being guided by his reactor team.'

I followed Tosh towards the rear of the cylinder. 'Where did you say the airlocks would be?' I asked.

'Stop right there,' said Ted.

I was about three metres from the rear bulkhead.

'Directly above and below you will be the airlocks to the landers and to your right will be the airlock to enter and leave the craft and to dock with the ISS or any other craft,' said Ted as he caught up with me.

Large circles outlined with white tape showed where the airlocks would be. We turned and walked towards the front, taking in the size of the ship.

'We'll not be short of space,' said Bill.

'Well, we're allowing additional capacity for Mary's beam-me-up device, if it ever becomes practical,' said Ted.

'Don't hold your breath,' said Mary. 'We're still killing dummies by dropping them from variable heights and if we get close to the ground there's a chance of materialising within it. Another explosion from that happened last Monday. We can't understand why it's so erratic, but we'll get there eventually.'

'And this is the cockpit?' asked Anna, tapping on the doorway which blocked our path.

'Well,' said Ted. 'More like a bridge, really. Go on in.'

Inside, it was very much like the cockpit of a jumbo jet, but much longer and with a larger diameter. It easily had room for five or six people and there was a mock-up of the controls for the targeting device. The piriform shape made moving around difficult owing to the sloping floor. Not important in freefall, of course.

'These are windows?' Mary asked, pointing at taped areas which surrounded the central nose.

'Yes,' said Ted. 'The aircraft division is constructing the cockpit and it will replace this mock-up. Again, as you will always be in freefall, the windows can completely surround the nose, giving a panoramic view.'

∞∞∞∞∞∞∞∞∞

Similar trips were made to SpaceX who were constructing the landers and fuel tanks to get back off the surface of any planet we visited. Oh for the casual planetary landings and take offs employed by the spacecraft in the fantasy worlds of *Star Wars* and *Star Trek*. If only we could magically invent their propulsion systems.

The landers were very similar in shape to the space shuttle, but a third of the size. It would be a tight fit for four of us to descend to the surface with enough provisions for a week, and enough equipment to carry out a professional scientific study. It had numerous external lockers to hold a tented shelter, buggy, inflatable boat for Trappist-1 missions, and much other essential scientific paraphernalia.

∞∞∞∞∞∞∞∞∞

I returned to our new home in Houston and a now much-enlarged Linda greeted me as I parked in the driveway of our new ranch-style bungalow.

58

'Hope you're not overdoing the gardening, darling,' I said as I pulled my overnight bag out of the trunk.

'No. Being very careful. Had a twinge last night. En says it's nothing to worry about and junior's entity will ensure I deliver at exactly the right time,' she said.

'And when is that likely to be? Has it changed?'

'En says it will still be the twenty-fifth, probably early afternoon.'

'She's that confident?' I asked and gave her a kiss.

'Absolutely, she says,' said Linda. 'Neil rang.'

'What did he want?' I asked as we crossed the threshold and I put my bag outside the bedroom door.

'He'd like to see you for a minute before your presentation to the congress people.'

I looked at my watch. One o'clock. 'Okay, let's get lunch and I'll head in to the JSC.'

'I thought I'd come with you,' she said.

'Okay. Let's get lunch at Luby's, and go on from there.'

∞∞∞∞∞∞∞∞∞∞∞

We entered Neil's office and he was around his desk in a flash, and giving Linda a hug. 'Lovely to see you,' he said, then stood back to look at her. 'Not long to go now?'

'Couple of weeks,' she said. As such a slight person, she looked huge but glowing in her paisley pattern dress.

'Can Linda sit in, or would you rather she didn't?' I asked.

'No problem at all. You're still an official NASA astronaut, Linda,' said Neil. 'No reason you shouldn't be vying with Anna to be number one pilot again some time.'

'What did you want me for?' I asked.

'I just thought you'd like to know that the Aldrin orbiting telescope has managed to produce a visible disc for Trappist-1G,' he said, handing over an eight by ten photograph which had the tiniest spot dead centre.

'Hmm. No detail,' I said and laughed.

'Ah,' said Neil, 'that's your job to obtain. It's why you're going.'

'It's 1G, not 1E?' I asked.

'Not got 1E yet, but it'll come and that will dispel Mary's worries about missing the target completely.'

'Neil,' said Linda. 'Something which has always bothered me – if 1E is targeted and the journey begins, why doesn't the ship end up where it was when it was targeted, rather than where it actually is? After all, the target is only where it was forty years ago.'

'Good question. Don't know the answer,' said Neil.

'Mary tells me,' I said, 'that the space-fold determines where it is at the time of targeting and it doesn't matter where it is when we arrive, because the whole dark universe moves, not the target. It is stationary in respect of the dark universe.'

'Right,' said Linda. 'Weird.'

'Indubitably,' said Neil.

∞∞∞∞∞∞∞∞∞∞

I'd given so many press and other briefings that you'd have thought it would be a walk in the park, but I was always more nervous standing in front of an expectant crowd than I ever was during landing or re-entry. Even sitting on the regolith on the moon that January day, my air running out, wondering if rescue would arrive in time, looking at the buggy buried in dust had been less nerve-racking than this. My entity calmed me, but I was still on edge.

The conference was in the boardroom at the Johnson Space Center. The plush room, with windows overlooking the complex, had a luxuriously thick pile carpet and stunning mahogany table holding complimentary notepads, pens, glasses and water jugs. This room was not used for management purposes, only for the most influential VIP conferences. Ten congressmen and women from the newly formed ISEC (Interstellar Space Exploration Committee) occupied most of the seats. Mine was at the opposite end to the committee chairwoman, Congresswoman Starling. Linda sat to my left and Mary on my right. She was there to add any technical detail required beyond the layperson's presentation I was giving to them today.

I introduced myself, Mary and Linda, then pressed a button on a handset which closed the blinds and brought down a screen behind me.

'This,' I stood, using my laser pointer to highlight an artist's impression of the starship, 'is our interstellar vessel. The globular reactor chamber is at the rear and the main cylinder has living quarters for up to eight people. The more aerodynamic piriform-shaped front is the bridge, in which the crew will be seated for the voyage.'

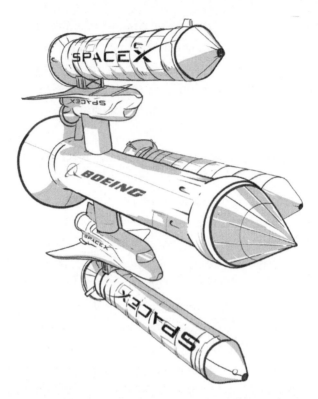

A hand shot up. 'Yes, Congressman Wilson?'

'You talk about a voyage, but I thought it was an instantaneous trip.'

Mary indicated that she wanted to answer and I waved her to go ahead. She stood up and said, 'Yes. We believe it will be instantaneous, but we also think we should be strapped into acceleration couches in case there is any physical shock to our bodies.'

Mr Wilson murmured his thanks, Mary sat down, and I continued, 'As you see, we have two landers attached either side of the main fuselage. These can hold four people, but could carry six in an emergency.'

'What sort of emergency would require that?' asked Congresswoman Blaney.

'If one of the landers were, for some reason, unable to lift off from a planet, a second lander could be sent to recover the crew. Hence the extra capacity,' I replied. I saw her nod that she understood. 'I should mention that only one lander will be used on each mission, the second being taken for just such an emergency recovery only.'

I continued, 'You will see that the dorsal sides or top sides of the landers are attached to the main hull cylinder by an access airlock. Attached to each of the lander's undersides is a large external fuel tank. There is a third fuel tank under the starship's main fuselage. These tanks contain liquid hydrogen and oxygen in separate compartments. They are mixed in the lander's engines to provide thrust. The landers also contain their own fuel supplies in the stubby wing areas as well as in the body of the craft. This fuel is enough for landing and for a few short trips around the landing area, up to five hundred miles in total depending on how much hovering is needed and the planet's gravity. They fly like vertical take-off jump jets. The landers, after atmospheric entry, coast in the same manner as the space shuttle, until they reach about two thousand metres. Then the engines are ignited to control altitude and direction until they arrive at the landing location.

'You see, here, at the bottom of the external fuel tanks, they have their own engines and integral legs. The entirety of the tank is covered in ultralight thermal tiles which mostly burn away during entry to the planet's atmosphere. At around two thousand metres, they come in for a controlled upright landing,' I said. An animation on the screen showed a fuel tank settling upright on the surface of a cartoon world.

'Now, after the missions on the surface, the lander uses the last of its fuel to position itself vertically. It approaches the fuel tank in that aspect, then descends so that the external fittings attach to the tank.'

'Sounds a tricky manoeuvre,' said Congresswoman Starling. 'And the tank landing, too.'

'There's no denying that it is difficult. SpaceX and Blue Origin have perfected the tank landings and have used the system on Earth reliably for a decade. These tanks are, of course, quite a lot larger than those they normally use for low-orbit capsule and resupply launches. Both have prototypes of these tanks and have landed them successfully several times after they were dropped from a jumbo jet. The attaching of the lander to the tank will be assisted by computers. The lander contains enough fuel to make several attempts, so not as risky as it might seem.'

Congresswoman Blaney asked, 'How does this spolding business work? Einstein said you can't exceed the speed of light, but that is what you are claiming to do here.'

I looked at Mary and she got to her feet. 'Without getting into too much detail, Congresswoman, let me say that general and special relativity still hold good in our normal universe. Have you heard of dark matter?'

'Yes,' said the Congresswoman, 'but I couldn't explain it.'

'No,' said Mary, 'it's very complex. Dark matter exists in large quantities. There may be more dark matter than normal matter in the universe. We cannot see it, but we know it is there because its mass affects galaxy rotation speeds. Einstein had never heard of it and didn't need to.

Normally it isn't important to us, but spolding makes use of it.

'The distance to Trappist-1 could not be covered by a journey in a Newtonian or an Einsteinian universe. It would take an impossibly long time. What we have to do therefore is move into the hidden or quantum universe, where we can interact with subatomic particles within dark matter. It is that which allows spolding to permit us to reach interstellar destinations.

'Think of it this way. In a Newtonian universe we can work out most of the mechanics of the solar system, but we require knowledge of Einstein's relativity to be able to make our global positioning devices function correctly. To fold space, we must leave this universe we all inhabit and enter a parallel dark or quantum universe, where spolding can be used to join distant places together.

'To summarise, we vanish from our universe into the quantum universe, make our journey, then return to our universe. Does that help?'

'Yes, it does,' said Congresswoman Blaney. 'It really does. So, we're not breaking the speed of light?'

'Absolutely not,' said Mary. 'We're temporarily going somewhere else where the speed of light is irrelevant. Einstein would have loved the symmetry of it all.'

Congressman Brenner said, 'Back to the mechanics of this journey. When we launch, say, an Orion, not only do we need a huge rocket, but also solid rocket boosters. How can we get out of Earth-type gravity with only a tank and the lander's engines?'

'Good question,' said Mary. 'That's where SpaceX comes into its own. They've been working with the Massachusetts Institute of Technology and they've used an MIT invention of an ultralight polymer and integrated it with aluminium. The landers and tanks are made from it. Our first starship isn't, but future vessels will be. It means that the tank feeding the lander engines can escape the Earth's gravity well.'

Congressman Gallagher said, 'If the fuel tank fails to land upright, what happens?'

'That is why we carry two spares,' I said. 'A second or even the third tank could descend if the first one crashes or is blown over in gales. If one craft is stranded on the surface, the second lander can make the descent. The external tanks will always be sent down first and will only be sent once we're satisfied with the weather conditions at the landing spot. No lander will descend to the surface until we know there is an upright fuel tank awaiting it for lift-off.'

Mary said, 'The moment a lander has touched down, cables will be ejected from the top of the tank. As soon as the manned lander has arrived, the first task of the crew will be to fix those cables to the ground to prevent the tank being toppled in high winds.'

'What happens to the tanks?' asked Congressman Gallagher.

'After take-off?' I asked. He nodded. 'When the lander attaches, a panel is opened in the fuselage and the computer connects the fuel pipes automatically. The first thing to happen after that is that the lander's tanks are filled. After lift-off, the entire assembly climbs to about seventy miles before jettisoning the empty tank. There is enough fuel in the lander to complete the rendezvous with the starship. The tank falls back to the surface.'

'That is what was worrying me,' said Congressman Gallagher. 'Not just what happens to them, but where they end up. We're littering the surface of alien worlds with our garbage and, potentially, contaminating those worlds with our bugs.'

'I can reassure you on the contamination,' said Mary. 'Everything in the starship and the outsides of the tanks and Rimors is fully disinfected in orbit. The heat tiles will crumble into dust in the presence of oxygen, even the low levels in the Martian atmosphere. The legs, tanks and other items will not contaminate, but will remain. Eventually, perhaps, they will be collected,' said Mary.

'So it is being considered?' the Congressman asked.

'It certainly is, Congressman,' I said, 'but we are still learning here, and we must be careful not to put so many constraints on these early expeditions, that they become impossibly complex.'

'Okay. Fair enough… for now,' he said.

Questions and answers continued for a further hour and I was grateful to have Mary present to deal with the more technical aspects and to describe the space-folding system which had now been officially designated as "spolding".

7 The Miraculous En

'It's time,' Linda said.

'It's started?' I asked in a panic, jumping up from my easy chair. Even though I knew we should expect it early afternoon on the twenty-fifth, it had still doubled my heart rate.

'En says we should call the midwife.'

I grabbed the phone and called Maureen, the woman who had been dealing with Linda's pregnancy. En had ensured that there hadn't been any complications and, worldwide, entities assisting in births had meant that infant and mother mortality during birth had become astonishingly rare.

Maureen arrived and gave Linda a thorough examination.

'She's asking if I'm ready,' said Linda.

'Who?' I asked. 'En?'

'Yes. She says, "any second". Help me to the bathroom.'

She was only in there for twenty seconds then returned to the bed. 'That was my waters. En saved me making a mess.'

The midwife was now busy and I sat beside Linda, holding her hand.

'Here it comes,' cried Maureen and I saw the head emerge, followed in seconds by the rest of a perfectly formed baby son.

'It's a boy,' I cried and looked at Linda. She was smiling.

'You not in pain?' I asked.

'No. None. En dealt with the pain and made the contractions much more efficient,' she said as she took the swaddled infant into her arms.

I took photographs.

'Maureen,' said Linda. 'The messy stuff's on the way.'

In short measure, Linda was cleaned up and the midwife on her way home. 'That was amazingly quick,' I said.

'Thank En for that,' Linda said. 'I'm not even puffed. Here, take Junior.'

I held my tiny son in my arms for a moment while Linda got up, took him back from me and walked through to the sitting room. We sat on the sofa. I felt useless, but exceedingly proud.

'En says everything is right with me,' said Linda. I watched her entity move from her neck to the baby. A few seconds later, it was back inside Linda. 'I had En double-check the baby for me. All one hundred per cent. We'd better choose a name.'

8 Test Flight

Our five-month-old son was in a stroller and I stood with him, gazing out of huge vertical windows in an observation area at the Kennedy Space Center.

A prototype lander, now named Rimor from the Latin for rummaging or exploring, stood on the apron at the beginning of a short runway. In the cockpit were Anna, Linda and Chi; Anna and Linda, NASA's two most senior astronaut pilots and Chi, the best from China, who'd now moved to the US and become a good friend and constant companion to Tosh. Strangely, they were both still hiding their romantic entanglement.

I was worried about Linda taking this test flight, but, for the umpteenth time, she assured me she was fully fit and that En had declared her fitter than she'd ever been in her life.

This was to be the first of the lander test flights.

A couple of hundred metres beyond the Rimor was a water-filled fuel tank, standing upright as if it had just landed on an alien world. The last manoeuvre they would undertake would be to dock to the tank as if preparing to lift off into space.

Jason slept, his bunny and teddy keeping him company while I listened in to the radio chatter between the Rimor and mission control in Houston.

'Okay, Anna, you have a go for engine start,' said Capcom, the designated communicator in Houston. The archaic name was still used despite the fact that the Rimor was not a capsule, but more like a conventional jet.

'Copy that,' Anna's voice crackled over the airwaves.

The three engines fired. A shimmering mist of primarily water vapour was ejected as hydrogen and oxygen combined. The Rimor began to accelerate and in seconds was airborne.

'That was smooth,' I heard Anna say as the rocket plane disappeared towards the Atlantic. Seemingly seconds later, she reported, 'That's Mach 1.' They were through the sound barrier.

'Looks good,' said Capcom.

'No vibration,' said Anna. 'Very smooth. Returning to base.'

In the distance, I saw the Rimor returning, a rapidly growing grey spot in the sky, on its way back to the Kennedy Space Center. I raised my binoculars and watched as it slowed on approach to a designated landing area which was about a mile away from the observation building. The two side engines began to swivel and, with the lander at a slightly upward facing angle of about twenty degrees, the Rimor became stationary for a few seconds, then softly descended.

'Touch down,' said Anna.

'We copy you down,' said Capcom.

'Engines cut,' said Anna.

There was a jumble of conversation between, Anna, Chi, Linda, Capcom and two NASA engineers as they discussed the Rimor's status, fuel consumption, external and internal temperatures et cetera.

'Ready for test two?' asked Capcom.

'Roger that,' said Chi, who had swapped pilot seats with Anna.

'You have a go for engine start, Chi,' said Capcom.

'Copy that,' said Chi.

I could hardly see any vapour at this distance, but I watched as the Rimor climbed vertically, nose slightly up, and then set off over the Atlantic again. A shorter trip this time and Chi brought the Rimor back towards the observation building, swivelling the engines to bring the craft to a halt, about thirty metres above the apron.

'Descending,' said Chi.

'Copy that,' said Capcom.

The Rimor very gradually, at less than walking speed, settled onto the concrete and the engines cut.

Once again, there was a babble of communication with Houston.

'First half of the final test for today. Ready?' asked Capcom.

'Copy that,' said Linda, now in the pilot's seat. 'Starting engines.' I crossed my fingers for her.

The Rimor rose into the air vertically then, at little more than cycling speed, it headed towards the dummy water-filled fuel tank. The tank needed to be stable, so water was used instead of fuel to provide the necessary ballast for the docking test flights.

Linda circled it tentatively. I was amazed at the manoeuvrability of the craft.

'Okay, Linda. Go for docking,' said Capcom. This was the most delicate part of the test flight.

'Copy that,' she said, and I saw the Rimor's nose rise until the lander was vertical, pointing towards the sky, balanced on the power from its three engines, ten metres above the ground and closing in on the sixty metre tall fuel tank.

'One metre,' said Linda.

'Copy that,' said Capcom.

The underside of the Rimor approached the tank extremely slowly.

'Contact,' said Linda.

The Rimor descended, but the movement was too insignificant to be seen from my location.

'Docked. Cutting engines to fifty per cent,' said Linda.

'Copy that,' said Capcom.

'Docking firm,' said Linda.

'Go for engine cut off,' said Capcom.

The Rimor was securely attached to the fuel tank, just above ground level. A perfect docking.

For the last part of the test, Anna was piloting again. The Rimor undocked and rose vertically, opening its distance from the tank until it could swing to the slightly upward facing orientation it needed to adopt to hover and descend.

The Rimor returned to the apron, landed, and the tests were over. The ultralight lander had proven its abilities.

Our planetary landing system had worked perfectly. There would be many additional test flights and, in a few weeks, a lift-off would be attempted with a fully loaded fuel tank.

Debriefing would take a couple of hours, so I pushed Jason into the coffee shop and enjoyed a latte and Danish.

The others joined me later and, after lunch, Linda flew Anna, Chi, Jason and me back to Houston. Now, if the starship were as successful as the exoplanet landing system, it looked as if we could be travelling to Mars and then Trappist-1 before Jason was two years old.

∞∞∞∞∞∞∞∞∞∞

Four SpaceX boosters took each of the two external tanks into orbit where they rendezvoused near the ISS. A further two tanks with the Rimors attached blasted into orbit as the final proof that the launch system would work on any Earth-sized exoplanet. Surface wind could be a problem and great care would be taken in selecting landing sites and their weather conditions.

The starship, now named Spirit, launched a week later. This was no simple task. Two external fuel tanks and six solid rocket boosters were needed to lift the weight of Spirit into orbit. The largest payload ever launched from planet Earth.

I gave Jason a cuddle and Linda and I had a long, meaningful hug before I left for my launch to the ISS.

'Stay safe,' Linda said. 'I won't be there to rescue you from the Martians.'

I promised I would.

The Crew Dragon would be piloted by Anna, with Bill, Chi, Mary, Tosh and me as passengers. Two Cygnus supply ships would follow us into orbit, packed with equipment and provisions for the first ever spolding expedition.

Teams of astronaut engineers, working out of the ISS, had fitted out Spirit, installed the reactor and welded the rear of the reactor compartment into place. It had been a complex job to carry out in freefall.

When we arrived in orbit, our first job was to attach to one of the outlying docking ports. Supplies were transferred, then we boarded and undocked from the ISS.

Five days later, we had docked with the two Rimor landers, one on each side, and then attached them to the two external fuel tanks. The third tank was attached to Spirit's underside. Now we were busy with the final checks and tests before we set off for the red planet.

Life on board Spirit was comfortable. It was spacious and even our personal cabins gave us room to move around without the continual congestion of the cubicles on the ISS.

Much of my time was spent checking every nook and cranny of all three craft. Checklist after checklist was completed until, finally, on the thirtieth of November 2031 we were given the all-clear to depart.

9 Departure

I'd had a long Skype call with Linda, and watched Jason playing in the background. I promised we'd be very careful and not take any unnecessary risks. In fact, the Mars mission would not see us completely cut off from Earth. The communication delay would be between four and twenty-four minutes. When we went to Trappist-1, there would be no communication at all.

This mission would only last a couple of weeks. It was really a test flight, checking that the design worked and the trips to the surface were viable. We knew they were, but it is always necessary to test and test and retest. Of course, Mars' gravity was only marginally over a third of that of Earth. Lift-off should be a very simple matter. It would be a different story when we got to the more massive worlds of Trappist-1.

Final checks were made and we prepared for departure. Would spolding really work and take us instantly to Mars?

'How's the targeting device doing, Mary?' I called to her. She was on the bridge.

She turned and floated into the doorway. 'Wonderful. Mars is sitting dead centre.'

'What's the timing?' asked Anna. 'Shall I orientate Spirit in readiness?'

'Yes. Think so,' said Mary.

'Okay, let's strap ourselves in and get this show on the road,' I said.

We all pulled ourselves through to the bridge and strapped into our seats. Tosh and Bill took the two rear couches. I sat in the centre of the front row with the communication and other computer screens in front of me giving our status. To my right, Anna was preparing to adjust our orbit and, to the left, Mary had but one screen, upon which we could see the crisp image of Mars. The final seat, attached to Anna's, was occupied by Chi. At a moment's notice Anna's instrumentation could be moved across in front of Chi to allow a smooth change of pilot in a crisis. None of us anticipated any crises but NASA insisted on the layout.

'Permission to change orbit?' asked Anna.

'You have a go for that,' said mission control.

I felt my weight move leftwards as Spirit rotated to the right. Pseudo-gravity pushed me gently back into my couch as the rotation stopped and we began to move away from the ISS. We needed five thousand kilometres of clear space between us and the ISS because some scientists believed the spolding process could create a gravitational shockwave. Mary insisted it was nonsense, but the safety margin was not too much of a cross to bear. Better safe than sorry.

Eventually, Spirit was in position. Mary's targeting device was pinpointing the Martian equator. Anna made the most delicate adjustments to our orientation and we were ready.

Our computer took over. It rotated us about our axis, one revolution every six minutes. Not enough to create weird gravitational effects or put too much strain on the connections between the tanks and Rimors, but just enough to ensure our centre of gravity truly was facing along the line which would take us from Earth to the red planet. The dream of so many famous authors was about to become a reality. A journey to Mars.

'Holding at five seconds,' said Anna.

A few seconds later, mission control said, 'You have a go to complete countdown. Godspeed Spirit.'

'Thank you, NASA,' I said.

Anna said, 'Ready, mark, four, three, two, one, zero!'

10 Hyperspace

No one knew what to expect. There had been dire warnings by some physicists that we'd be crushed back into our seats, or instantly killed by the shock of entering the hidden or dark universe. At Anna's call of 'zero!' we found out.

I was still alive. I did feel that I was glued to my couch. I couldn't move my arms, but it wasn't owing to gravity. It was something in the very environment of the ship. Air seemed to have solidified. It immobilised me. I couldn't move.

Just seconds later it ended. I was thrown forward, but the seatbelts restrained me. We were there. The gorgeous rusty red orb, with one of its ice caps turned to face us, was hanging above the cockpit.

'Wow!' said Bill.

'Ninety-eight thousand miles. Adopting a high orbit,' said Anna, and we experienced several minutes thrusting.

'Everything stable?' asked Mary.

'Eighty-eight thousand mile orbit now stable,' replied Anna. 'Everyone okay?'

Tosh, Chi, Bill and I all replied in the affirmative.

'Okay. Take us down to two hundred and fifty miles,' I said.

'Braking burn in three, two, one, fire,' said Anna.

To us, it seemed to be an acceleration, not braking. Spirit was falling out of its orbit, but gaining speed as it headed for a new orbit at a height of about two hundred and fifty miles.

I felt several orbital adjustments as Anna stabilised us at the new altitude. 'Orbit achieved,' she said.

'Hello, NASA. Spirit here. We are in orbit two hundred and fifty miles above Mars. Spolding drive worked perfectly, no ill effects. Out,' I said. It would be more than twenty minutes before we could receive a reply.

'Okay,' I said to the crew. 'Anna, Mary, Tosh and I will take the Rimor. Let's get prepared. Chi, can you prepare to send the fuel tank down to Perseverance Valley. Try to land it about six hundred metres from the Opportunity Rover.'

'Will do,' said Chi.

Our first destination would be to the last resting place of the Opportunity Rover which was declared dead in February 2019. To make best use of our test flights, the first task would be to find the rover, replace its batteries and clean dust off the solar panels.

Chi and Anna sat side by side in the Rimor with Bill, Tosh and me watching over their shoulders. Mary was at the main computer console in Spirit's cockpit to ensure the correct landing data was provided. Preparations took about forty minutes.

'Okay. Systems ready,' Chi said. 'About to separate and begin atmospheric entry.' Chi armed the switches for separation from tank lander number one.

'Armed and ready,' she said.

'Okay, go for separation,' I said.

We heard a mechanical clunk from beneath us and the huge tank of propellant drifted forwards and away.

It was an odd sensation looking out of the Rimor's cockpit. In front, apparently above us, was Spirit, stretching away to the fore. The orange tank which had been strapped beneath us also pointed forward, but was now moving away. Soon it was lost to our vision. This didn't affect Chi or Anna. In front of them were two sets of controls and two video screens, both showing the bottom of the tank from different cameras on the sides of it.

'Rotating,' said Chi.

'Copy,' said Anna as the tank swivelled and came back into view in front of the cockpit, turning to be ninety degrees to Spirit.

Controlling it remotely, Chi turned it so that it faced rear-end to its direction of travel. More thrusters caused it to move away from us until it reached a safe distance, far enough away from Spirit that even a catastrophic accident wouldn't harm the starship.

'Looking good,' said Chi.

'Safe distance,' said Anna. 'Mary, we're oriented for descent, just give Chi a go when we're in the right location.'

'Roger that, Anna,' said Mary over the intercom. 'Around ten minutes. I'll give you a "mark" at one.'

'Copy that,' said Anna.

Tank one now hung in space before us like a giant orange cigar tube, with the planet beyond, the daylight dividing line moving to the left beneath us.

'Get ready,' said Mary. 'Five, four, three, two, one, *mark!*'

Anna snapped a switch to start the countdown clock. 'Countdown running,' she said.

How long can a minute last? This one seemed interminable as the clock read thirty seconds, then, seemingly an hour later it said twenty. They say a watched pot never boils, well that is exactly how it seemed to us.

What felt to me like an hour later, Chi said, 'Ten seconds.'

She counted down to zero and Anna pressed the "FIRE" button on her panel. A haze appeared at the tail of the tank as it began its braking manoeuvre and moved away from us, relentlessly gaining speed as it commenced the precarious descent into Martian atmosphere.

As the tank disappeared from view, I intently studied the two monitors in front of the women pilots. There was vibration, but not excessive. Mars seemed to be getting no closer, but I realised that was an illusion.

Chi turned the tank through one hundred and eighty degrees. The landing blast was complete, now the front and sides of the tank would take the full venom of atmospheric entry. On the monitors, we watched flanges opening, widening the tank towards its base to protect the legs and engine from the heat being generated during its dash through the upper atmosphere. At the top of the tank, although we couldn't see it, the heat shield would have inflated to protect the vessel from the bulk of the early heat. So far, so good.

As the temperatures built up, Anna revolved the tank again to spread the searing heat, so that it was continually turning a different section of its tile-covered hull to the direction of descent. We could see the whole thing glowing, more one side than the other, but each face taking its share of the punishment as the revolutions continued.

'Entering blackout,' said Anna.

The video images flickered and vanished. The tank was now autonomous for fifteen minutes or so as the ionisation around the craft prevented radio signals from reaching Spirit.

'Three minutes,' said Anna.

There was nothing we could do at this point. We had no telemetry from the tank and were relying on the SpaceX scientists having got the calculations right.

'Six minutes,' said Anna.

I thought back to the first tank re-entry tests the previous year. The second test had been perfect, the fully laden tank descending vertically into the Nevada desert and touching down as steady as a rock. There had been huge cheers throughout mission control.

'Ten minutes,' said Anna.

The first test flight, however, had not gone at all well. The descent jets were doing their job, but the landing legs had been badly damaged by the heat of re-entry because the flanges had not fully opened. The tank hit the ground, overbalanced and the media were treated to an absolutely enormous explosion as nine hundred thousand gallons of liquid oxygen and hydrogen unexpectedly found themselves meeting as the tank ruptured. It was nothing less than spectacular.

'Thirteen minutes,' said Anna.

Apparently, it had been caused by the flanges, which we had been watching on our monitors, not opening properly and being stripped away by re-entry drag. The specification on the securing struts was changed for the second flight. SpaceX had done their job. Tests two, three and four were perfect.

'Fifteen minutes,' said Anna.

Mars had a much thinner atmosphere than Earth, so atmospheric entry should be much simpler. With space flight, however, nothing was ever certain.

All of a sudden, the monitors flickered into life and we were watching the descent. The sky was no longer black but dark blue behind the tank which was still heading nose first towards the surface.

'A weak jet stream's buffeting the tank,' said Anna.

'Still stable. We'll be through it soon,' said Chi.

'Inflatable heat shield gone,' said Anna. 'Auto rotation any moment.'

The monitors showed the huge tank swivelling until we saw the land beneath. The flanges which protected its legs were blackened and many heat resistant tiles had broken away from the main structure.

'Ready for sloughing,' said Anna.

The protective skirt of flanges around the tank broke away and vanished in the lower atmosphere. This triggered the remaining heat tiles to break off from the bottom upwards like one of those domino cascades. We could see them being shed as the tank descended. Soon they were all gone as the bare lightweight polymer-aluminium tank neared the surface.

'Five thousand metres,' said Chi.

'On target,' said Anna.

The tank was now wavering from side to side as its motors fired short bursts to maintain its vertical orientation. On the monitor, the surface rushed towards us.

'Two thousand metres,' said Chi.

Now we could see the landing site, the valley where Opportunity had met its end. The landing engines were at fifty per cent power, slowing the descent and maintaining its vertical orientation.

'One hundred metres,' said Chi.

'*Touchdown!*' said Anna. 'Motors shutdown. Standing vertical. Sensors read very slight breeze.'

Dust or sand cleared with the motors now off. The cameras swivelled into horizontal mode and we could see the Martian desert stretching away to the horizon. The tank was on the ground and all was set for the first humans to join it and set foot on the red planet's surface.

11 Red Planet

Being the first person to take a step on the moon was a huge deal. Neil and Buzz actually argued over it because the commander on previous flights was always the one who did *not* do the EVAs. Buzz therefore thought that he should be first down the ladder. NASA decided, however, that it must be Neil. Before the event, most people considered that both Neil and Buzz would jointly be the first men on the moon and so they were, but Buzz knew that was a naïve point of view and he was proven right after the event. Neil, despite trying to shrug off his importance, became far more of a celebrity than Buzz because he took that first step. One of those few people in history who will never be forgotten. No one knows who Vasco da Gama's right-hand man was, nor Cook's nor Columbus'. Few know the name of the second astronaut in space after the immortalised Gagarin. It was actually Titov, but when you Google "Who was the second man in space?", you are given Gus Grissom which shows how partisan a Google search can be. Now we were about to set foot on Mars. NASA had given me strict instructions about who should be first down the ladder on this occasion.

'The first excursion will be Anna, Tosh, Mary and me,' I said.

'We have a twenty-four hour hold first,' said Anna. 'We need to wait to ensure the landing site is stable and the tank remains upright.'

'Yes, of course,' I said, acknowledging the protocol.

∞∞∞∞∞∞∞∞∞∞∞

The next day, we finished our checks in the Rimor and were ready for the descent. We had enough stores for two weeks, but this expedition was strictly a test flight. The cupboards and external lockers were filled with scientific equipment, containers, microscopes and many electronic sensors and scanners which would be left in an inflatable shelter as a cache for future missions. We'd taken lightweight pressure suits similar to those we used for brief excursions on the moon.

Anna occupied the pilot's seat with me in the command slot. Behind us were Tosh and Mary. The Rimor was cramped even with four, and its cargo of equipment and stores were more important than extra astronauts. Chi and Bill were not going to get their share of fame on this mission.

'Separating,' said Anna.

There was a metallic noise from where the airlock above us separated from Spirit. Through the windows, we could see that we were drifting away.

Using the manoeuvring jets, Anna applied some gentle thrust to take us far enough away from Spirit that we would not damage the starship if there was any explosive mishap. SpaceX, Boeing and Blue Origin made our ships as safe as was possible, but operating in orbit, whether around Earth or some alien world, always had its dangers and the vacuum of space is most unforgiving.

'One mile,' said Anna. 'Orientating.'

'Three, two, one, mark!' said Chi over the radio.

Anna hit the automatic countdown. Once again we were waiting. In one minute we'd be on our way to the surface.

'Zero,' announced Anna, and we felt the main engines start. They would fire for twenty seconds, slowing us down and causing us to enter Mars' atmosphere.

Once the engines cut off, Anna swung us around and that put the hull in the correct position for atmospheric entry. The Rimor began to vibrate. Anna had already landed an earlier version of this craft on Earth more than once, so she was experienced in what was to come. The vibrations increased as the hull bit into Mars' thin atmosphere.

'Much less vibration than Earth entry,' Anna said.

Flames and sparks flew past the windows as the tiled heat shield began to vaporise, burning away to protect its precious cargo. Each Rimor only made a single landing. Reducing the lift-off weight to a minimum was a priority. By the time we landed, only remnants of the tiles would remain and one of our jobs would be to knock them off before lift-off.

We began to feel some of the atmospheric entry heat. The ultralight polymer-aluminium hull was not as effective as a space shuttle's, but it would serve its purpose.

Still coasting, we were through the atmospheric entry episode and now gliding down from twenty thousand metres.

'Spirit, Rimor here, do you copy? Over,' said Anna.

'We copy you,' replied Chi. 'Any problems?'

'No, very smooth. Passing the equivalent of Mach 2.'

We descended rapidly towards the surface, so familiar from our studying of detailed images from the Mars orbiter.

'Under the equivalent of Mach 1,' said Anna.

Our landing site was to the north. We couldn't yet see Perseverance Valley, but knew more or less where it was in relation to other landmarks.

'Five thousand metres,' said Anna. 'Landing site visible.'

'Hey, I can see the tank,' said Mary from behind me.

The orange structure stood out against the ochre landscape below, looking for all the world like a pin in a three-dimensional map.

'Powering up,' said Anna, and we all waited for the crucial feel of the engines coming into play.

'Under power,' said Anna, and we all breathed a sigh of relief.

'Copy that,' said Chi from orbit.

The Rimor was now in controlled flight, heading for the giant orange tank.

'Less stable in flight than it was on Earth,' said Anna.

'A problem?' I asked.

'No. It's okay.'

'Probably the thinner atmosphere,' said Mary.

'I'm sure you're right,' said Anna as she concentrated on juggling the wing surfaces to keep us on the best vector.

Suddenly, the nose of the Rimor rose and we came to a halt in mid-air, maybe fifteen metres above the ground. We descended like a Harrier Jump Jet onto a flat area, approximately one hundred metres from the tank which sat majestically before us.

'Engines cut,' said Anna.

'Copy that,' said Chi.

'Venting engines. Stable landing. The Rimor has landed on Mars,' said Anna.

'Congratulations,' said Chi.

'Well done, all,' added Bill.

As dust settled, in front of us the vista of a reddish brown world appeared, so familiar from the images sent back by numerous rovers.

'Stay, no stay?' asked Anna.

'Stay,' said Mary, looking at the consumable's console.

'Stay,' said Chi, from Spirit.

'Stay,' I confirmed.

'Lift-off systems changed to standby,' said Anna. 'NASA, I know you won't hear this for ten minutes, but the Rimor has landed.'

'Okay, prepare for EVA,' I said.

'Temperature minus eighteen C,' said Tosh. 'No perceptible wind.'

We unstrapped ourselves and began to don the lightweight pressure suits. Not easy in the cramped cockpit, but eventually we had all sealed ourselves and checked each other's suit integrity. The backpacks were the size of two average briefcases and fitted over our shoulders very much as a camping backpack.

'All sealed and checked?' I asked.

'Yes,' came from each of the others.

'Opening the inner airlock door,' I said.

We crowded into the small chamber which was no larger than a couple of shower cubicles. A very tight fit for four of us.

'Inner door sealed,' I said.

'Who goes down first?' asked Tosh.

'I have strict instructions for that,' I said.

I pressed a red button on the wall. The outer door swung away from the ship and Tosh mounted the NASA television camera onto the doorway, pointing down the steps to provide a permanent record of the event.

They all looked at me.

'Mary, you first,' I said.

'Really?' she said in surprise.

'NASA insisted,' I said.

'Wow! What do I say?' she asked.

'Your call, Mary,' I said.

She moved slowly into the opening and I watched her feeling for the top step. The first human to set foot on Mars would be a woman. She stopped near the bottom of the ladder.

'I'm thinking,' she said, as an excuse for her lack of movement. 'Armstrong had ages to think up his clever first words on the moon.'

She stepped down onto the soil of the previously elusive red planet. Humankind had finally arrived.

Mary looked around her, taking in the scene. The rest of us waited with bated breath. 'Apollo might have represented a giant leap for mankind, but this is a stepping stone to the rest of the universe!'

'Very nice,' said Anna. 'I hope Tosh remembered to switch on the camera!'

'Ha! Ye of little faith!' he scoffed.

'I only had the time it took me to climb down to think of it, sorry,' Mary said. 'Never thought it would be me. Thought Mark would have had something planned.'

I laughed. 'Glad I didn't have that pressure, but I would like to say that I hope the story of our landing will be worthy of being added to Bradbury's *Martian Chronicles*.'

Tosh said, 'First thing I did was look out of the window expecting a village green and chocolate box cottages!' We all chuckled.

Anna shut the airlock behind us. Once we were all down the ladder, we looked down at our feet, marvelling at where we were.

'No aliens, though,' said Tosh, as he set up four cameras at each side of the Rimor to film everything we did. 'Let's raise a glass later to all the sci-fi writers who described mankind's numerous first steps on Mars.'

'Where's Opportunity?' asked Mary.

Anna looked around then pointed to the south. 'There it is,' she said.

In the distance, at least half a mile away, the rover sat, covered in so much dust that it was almost lost in the scene.

'First things first,' I said. 'Tosh, bring the pneumatic stapler. We need to secure the tank.'

We walked towards it, Tosh carrying the device which would fix the tethers to the ground using titanium staples. The tank was in good condition. The tiles had sloughed off as required and, despite a few tiles resembling scabs, the surface was now pure polymer-aluminium. Its light as a feather structure was full of fuel and ready for blast-off. The jet assembly was intact and undamaged and the legs were in good condition. They would be left behind to save weight when we lifted off.

'It's tilting at four degrees,' said Anna, using her tablet as a spirit level.

'Okay, let's jack it up first,' I said.

'Capcom here. Thanks for those first words, Mary. Several billion were watching live.'

Anna and Tosh used manual adjusters to raise legs one and two to straighten the tank.

'Are the images okay?' asked Tosh.

'Vertical now,' said Anna.

Three tethers hung down from the top of the tank. One at a time we took them to their full extent, maybe forty metres from the tank. Here, Tosh stapled them to the ground. The whole exercise took about forty minutes. Part way through, NASA confirmed the images were perfect.

Using my tablet, I signalled the device on the top of the tank and it took up the slack so that the tethers were taut. Another crucial task undertaken ready for our departure.

Back at the Rimor, Tosh pulled a case of tools out of an external locker. I carried the batteries and we set off towards Opportunity. Mary followed us with a soft brush while Anna stayed behind to examine the ship for any damage and to deal with the communications from NASA. The communication delay made it most difficult to keep track of questions and answers. Most of the heat tiles had been stripped away by the force of the wind in the lower atmosphere and Anna removed those that remained.

'All the brackets and fittings survived the journey,' she said over the radio. 'A few tiles to remove, that's all.'

'Copy that,' I said as we walked across the rock-strewn Martian surface towards the Opportunity rover.

'It's covered in dust,' said Mary.

'Very gentle with the solar panels,' said Tosh.

As we got closer, we could see a build-up of light dust against the northern side of the wheels from the last dust storm. The solar panels were completely obscured by the rusty coloured regolith. No wonder it had stopped responding. It was the same with the camera too.

The rover had three wheels on each side, two solar panels on each side and another in the centre. They formed the top of the rover. Protruding above them was the Pancam mast which held a high resolution camera and also monochrome navigation and hazard cameras. To the rear of the mast was the low-gain antenna, like a pipe sticking up. Adjacent to that was the circular high-gain antenna, again coated with dust.

I gently rubbed my finger over the side of the high-gain antenna. The dust almost seemed as if it was caked onto the surface.

'I wonder if there is occasional moisture in the atmosphere,' I said. 'Look how the dust appears to have adhered to the surfaces.'

'Yes,' said Tosh. 'Certainly looks as if the dust has clung to the metal and glass. No humidity showing on my instruments at the moment, but there could be enough overnight to cause that effect, perhaps. Mind you, it's been sitting here immobile for more than a decade.'

Mary began a gentle brushing of the Pancam mast, then the antennae, before starting on the left side solar panels. Meanwhile, Tosh was lying on his back, his backpack still connected but lying to one side, under the right-hand panels where he had access to the two batteries. Each had eight cells. It was a tight fit and the connections were a little tricky, but after about forty-five minutes he'd replaced both.

'Hello, mission control,' I said on the NASA channel. 'Tosh has replaced the batteries and we'd like you to see if you can check for signs of life in the rover.'

Mary finished gently brushing off the panels. If the rover could be brought back to life, it could be good for several more years of operation.

I looked at my watch. By now Anna had joined us and NASA should have received my message and replied.

The Pancam rotated. 'Wow,' I shouted, 'we did it. It's operating.'

'Hello, Mark,' said Capcom. 'We've sent a command to rotate the camera. If you see that happen, please stand in front of it and we'll be able to see you. Shame about this delay.'

The four of us stood in direct view and waved.

'We'd better get out of the way because they're sure to want to try moving it. Well done, guys,' I said.

'Great group pic, guys,' said Capcom twenty minutes later. 'Neil's sent it to the media.'

'Acknowledged,' I said. 'We've returned to the lander so that we're out of the way if you want to try manoeuvring it.'

So began a period of scientific work. Rock samples, dust samples, some drilling and splitting of sedimentary layers in search of any clues about life. Meantime, Anna and I unloaded all of the supplies and equipment which were to be left behind for future missions.

This involved erecting a sturdy canvas tent which had been stored in an exterior locker, and pegging it down with heavy-duty staples.

It had been a long day and relieving ourselves of the spacesuits back inside was a pleasure, at first, but smelly until all the soiled diapers were bagged to be ejected when we returned to orbit. We had a nearby area where we could bury other waste. Sleeping in such close proximity in the Rimor was also less than ideal.

Anna flew us to the top of Olympus Mons on the second day. We collected samples of the volcano's most recent activity. Later analysis might inform us for how long it had been extinct. What an unbelievable experience it was for me, as a geologist, to stand on the summit of the largest volcano in the solar system.

We visited one of the dried riverbeds on our third day. Tosh found water ice at a depth of two metres. The team back at mission control were thrilled at the news. It meant that both fuel and oxygen could be manufactured on Mars with the right equipment. Mary helped me take cores from the same area. The presence of water offered hope of finding life. Tosh used his microscope, but try as he might, he could not see any living microbes or even their fossils in the samples. We'd need to return to Earth to examine the cores in more detail. Tosh did collect a rock which had a surface heavily pitted with burst air bubbles. It would be placed into a special vacuum container for return to Earth. Scientists would then calculate its age, cut it open under controlled conditions and analyse the ancient Martian air. It might throw light on how much thicker the atmosphere may have been when the rock was formed, and the nature of the constituent gases.

We visited the crash site of the British probe, Beagle, on our fourth day. The impact had clearly been extremely violent. We bagged a few pieces of the probe so that they could be tested for the long-term effects of radiation on manmade objects sitting on the Martian surface.

Eventually we returned to base later that afternoon and began transferring equipment we'd never use again, into the canvas tent.

'Does that look vertical to you?' asked Anna, pointing at the fuel tank.

'Yes, I think so,' I said.

Anna returned to the Rimor for her tablet and checked.

'One point five degrees off,' she said.

We both walked over and examined the tethers securing the tank.

'It's not taut,' I said.

'The tank must be tipping. Tosh, you hearing this?' said Anna.

'Copy that, Anna. I'll bring the stapler,' he replied.

Anna and I returned to the opposing legs and carefully jacked them up until the tank was vertical. Strangely, the tethers on this side were still tight, so that meant the ground itself could be moving under the tank.

97

'I've re-stapled that tether, Anna,' said Tosh.

'Copy that,' she said. 'The ground on this side must not be as solid as the other. I'd be happier if our docking fixings were on the other side. Adding our mass to the side of the direction of slip could add to the problem.'

'Yes, and the tethers will no longer be steadying the tank when we dock,' I said.

Anna spent the next ten minutes reporting the problem to Bill, Chi and NASA. NASA's suggestion was that we bring forward departure to that afternoon instead of the next day. They told us that Opportunity's cameras were swivelled around to watch us lift off. It was part of the plan that if the rover could be revived, it could film the event.

'Okay,' said Anna. 'Let's trim the craft ready for docking and lift-off.'

'Chi, how are we in relation to orbit requirements?' asked Mary.

'Any time in the next four hours will do. We'll come and get you in orbit if necessary,' said Chi.

Mary said, 'You know, it would be better if we could release the tethers remotely once we are attached to the tank. I'll ask SpaceX to look at that when we get back.'

'Sounds like a plan,' I said. 'There might need to be more on the side opposite docking though. Don't like the idea of trying to dock with cables in the way.'

'No. Good point,' said Mary.

Fifteen minutes later, Tosh reported that all external lockers were empty, save those which contained rock and regolith samples. Anything not required had been put into the storage tent and we were ready to leave. Anna, Tosh and Mary climbed aboard.

Still standing on the surface, I pressed a button on my tablet and watched the tethers disconnect from the top of the tank and tumble slowly under the weak Mars gravity to the desert below. I tried to envisage any problem with Mary's suggestion for doing this from inside the Rimor.

'Tethers released,' I said.

'Copy that,' said Anna, who was already in her pilot's seat.

We climbed aboard, quickly donned our flight suits, and strapped ourselves into the seats. This was to be the most critical part of the mission and, potentially, with the ground not being as firm as we would have liked, the most dangerous.

12 Emergency

'Everyone secure?' I asked and got three affirmatives. 'Okay, Anna. Take command.'

The engines started and Rimor lifted off vertically. It swung around and we could see the tank standing before us. Now the Rimor was manoeuvred into a vertical position. Anna could no longer see the tank and she activated the automatic dock system. Although it could be done manually, the automatic system was faster.

The Rimor approached the tank. My nerves tensed as I worried about the force of the engines causing more land slippage beneath us.

'Warning. Tank no longer vertical,' said the computer.

Anna made no comment, watching the external cameras intently as the Rimor came up against the tank and slid downwards into its docking brackets.

'Warning. Tank no longer vertical,' repeated the computer.

'Angle, computer?' asked Anna.

'One point seven degrees,' said the computer.

'Docking brackets locked,' said the computer, then after about fifteen seconds it added, 'Fuel hoses connected.'

'Computer, begin fuel pumping,' said Anna.

'Pumping commencing.'

The Rimor's tanks were now filling with fuel from the main tank. We could not lift off until they were at least partially replenished, otherwise we'd have no manoeuvring capability in orbit.

'Warning. Tank angle increasing. Now two point two degrees,' said the computer.

'Computer, how much fuel in the Rimor?' asked Anna.

'Sixty per cent. Tank now at three point six degrees and increasing,' warned the computer.

'We're toppling,' said Anna. 'Prepare for lift-off. Computer, seal tank valves and disconnect the hoses.'

All of a sudden, the movement of the tank became obvious. I gripped my armrests. The entire assembly was falling and we'd be underneath it. I heard a gasp from Bill, but Anna was as cool as ever. Nothing fazed her. When the whole stack hit the desert, the lightweight tank would rupture. The oxygen and hydrogen would meet in our exhaust and we'd be consumed in the fireball. We'd certainly not survive. A childhood fear of fire passed through me. Would it be quick? I gripped the seat tighter.

'Tank valves disconnected. Tank now in continual motion. Currently eight degrees,' said the computer.

'I'm firing,' said Anna.

I saw her finger jab the red button on the screen before her and we felt the ignition and power of the tank's motors joining our own. Lift-off began.

'Warning,' said the computer. 'Lift-off not vertical. Assembly at seventeen degrees.'

We had left the ground. Seventeen degrees was certainly enough for us to feel as the ship started to gain velocity. I could see the Martian desert through the windows as we were now on our backs. We should be vertical. Automatic engine controls tried to bring us back to vertical. Not a word from Anna who I could see hitting buttons, bringing up displays, looking for solutions for problems yet to materialise. This was *not* a normal lift-off.

'Assembly at fifteen degrees,' said the computer, meaning that the gimballing engines had created some recovery. *Could we regain the correct angle of ascent? My grip on the seat didn't lessen.*

Anna broke her silence. 'Altitude one thousand metres. The problem is that the angle is changing our trajectory. We won't be able to achieve the planned orbit,' said Anna, as if it was no more important than being late for lunch.

I sensed the force of the acceleration. 'Make any good orbit, Anna, and Spirit will come and get us,' I managed to say more coolly than I felt.

'Assembly at eighteen degrees,' said the computer.

'We're losing it,' said Anna. 'The angle is too great for the engines to compensate. Be prepared for emergency separation.'

I could see it was all wrong. The desert almost filled the scene above my head. We weren't going to make it.

'Assembly at thirty degrees. Danger. Danger!' said the computer. I guessed I wasn't the only one hanging onto my seat with both hands.

'Revolve us, computer,' said Anna, still the epitome of the test pilot.

I watched the live schematic on the upper screen in the control panel. The ship was revolving, bringing the Rimor around to the top side of the tank from its previous position hanging beneath.

As commander, I was in an unenviable situation. Anna was without doubt in trouble. I couldn't help her. The fear was tangible. I saw Tosh snap his visor shut. We weren't getting to orbit. Anna was using the tank to gain as much height as she could, but at an angle of over thirty degrees the ratio of downrange to altitude was slipping and fuel must be running low by now. The tank jets were designed to maintain a fixed flight plan, but this was way off. Anna shut her visor, and that did worry me. I heard Mary close hers and snapped mine shut too.

When the rotation completed, the computer warned of fifty degrees and Anna shouted, 'Brace for emergency separation.' Still professional, as in control as it was possible to be. I wondered how often she had practiced this in simulation.

Crunch time. My heart rate was through the roof. This was it. Anna must disconnect before we'd reached a sufficient altitude to achieve orbit. Perhaps she had enough left in the Rimor to see us through the crisis. I didn't know. This was not a scenario I'd been involved in during simulation. I'd have aborted a couple of minutes after lift-off.

'Assembly at sixty degrees. Tank fuel at ten per cent,' said the computer.

'Emergency undock!' said Anna. If it was possible, the rest of us gripped our seats even more tightly.

She hit the button which would separate us from the tank. A loud clunk sounded from outside, the Rimor shook, and we felt it accelerate now it was free of the external tank.

'Computer, fuel?' she said.

'Fifty-four per cent,' said the computer.

'Computer, what orbit can we achieve with that?' Anna asked.

'Between forty-eight and fifty-five miles, Anna,' replied the computer.

'Chi. Do you have a fix on us?' asked Anna.

'Copy that. We do. Have been keeping our noses out of your problems, but monitoring them,' said Chi over the radio.

'Can you rendezvous at forty-eight miles?' asked Anna.

'Bit low. Add ten and we'd be fairly certain,' said Chi.

'Can't be more specific,' said Anna. 'Either you can rendezvous at forty-eight miles or I'll have to abort and return to the surface.'

'What does Mary think?' asked Chi. 'I'm dubious of any rendezvous under fifty-eight miles.'

'I'm with Chi,' said Mary. 'If Spirit descends to forty-eight miles, it might not have the manoeuvring power to get back into orbit.

'Computer, fuel?' asked Anna.

'Forty per cent and falling at ten per cent per minute,' said the computer.

I could imagine the calculations flying through Anna's and Chi's minds. I felt helpless. I couldn't help with this and Mary was agreeing with Chi. Anna must make a decision before fuel reached twenty per cent. One minute had gone. Anna had less than sixty seconds to decide whether to abort or try a rendezvous which was likely to endanger both craft. Should I step in and call for the abort?

Five seconds later, Anna said, 'Aborting!'

The power ceased and the Rimor was suddenly in a version of free fall that we all recognised from the vomit-comet back on Earth.

'Ah, wings biting,' she said.

The stomach-sinking sensation passed and we were now heading down towards the surface once more with the engines off.

'Twenty thousand metres,' said Anna.

'Where are we headed?' I asked.

'We're going in the general direction of Gusev crater. There's plenty of flat terrain there,' said Anna, as if she was just avoiding congestion on the journey home.

'Ten thousand metres,' said Anna. 'Prepare for engine re-ignition.'

We were still coasting, but, unlike the space shuttle, we had no perfectly flat runway to aim for, so the engines would fire at about five thousand metres and we'd land as if returning from one of our excursion trips. This time, however, we had no way to leave the planet and our lives would be in the hands of Chi who would land a second tank close to our location.

I felt the thrust of the engines as they fired up and breathed a sigh of relief. At least Anna was in control of our fate again.

'Under power,' said Anna.

The next ten minutes were less stressful. We'd done this before. Anna chose the flattest area within Gusev crater that she could find and Rimor settled gently back onto the surface of Mars.

'Engines cut,' said Anna.

'Copy that,' said Chi.

'Venting engines. Stable landing. Rimor has landed,' said Anna. 'Computer, fuel?'

'Seven per cent, Anna,' said the computer.

We all knew that five per cent was the bare minimum to fire up the engines to approach and dock with a tank, so we were close to minimums. No room for error. We'd only get one shot at it.

'Well done, Anna,' said Tosh. A rare compliment indeed from the usually belligerent and stern doctor, perhaps showing that he wasn't immune to apprehension and fear after all.

I breathed a sigh of relief and seconded the praise, as did Mary.

'We'd better get some rest,' I said. 'No point getting suited up for the surface this late in the day.'

'No, but I'll stay on duty,' said Mary, 'in case Chi needs us.

13 Anxious Times

I awoke as the weak dawn sunshine illuminated the inside of the Rimor. I was immediately anxious about our unexpected isolation. The landing systems required a method of lifting off to be available before the Rimor touched down. Our method of returning to orbit was now lying somewhere in the Martian desert, almost certainly having exploded on impact if the tank had ruptured. Fortunately, there were a number of plans to deal with this eventuality, but they were all less than ideal.

The computer told us that we had enough fuel to dock with the next tank when it arrived. Two external tanks were still attached to Spirit and also a spare Rimor. If we hadn't enough fuel to dock, the other Rimor could come to our rescue, but that would reduce the backups to zero. First things first. Chi would have to pilot the second tank down to our location. All her calculations were being checked by NASA. Our fuel was sufficiently tight that we could not afford a lengthy journey to rendezvous with the tank.

'Rimor, come in, over,' said Chi over the radio.

'Copy you,' said Anna.

'This is a little more complicated than we expected,' said Chi. 'Your location requires Spirit to change to a polar orbit in order to get the tank close to your location. NASA are currently checking my calculations.'

'Send me a copy, please,' said Mary.

'On its way,' said Chi. 'Can you do an EVA and check that the ground is strong enough to take the weight of the tank? Find a section of granite bedrock rather than sandstone if you can, and send me the coordinates.'

'We left the drill at Perseverance Valley,' said Tosh. 'We will only be able to make a visual judgement call.'

'Did you hear that, Chi?' I said.

'Will have to do,' she replied.

I said, 'Let's get suited up guys.'

Forty minutes later, we were ready to descend to the surface. Mary had her head buried in calculations, so it was Anna, Tosh and me who climbed down into Gusev crater.

'Desolate,' said Tosh, surveying the scene. 'What's this material we're standing on?'

'Basalt,' I replied, 'but there are hollow areas of compressed regolith which would not be so stable. What's the plan, then?'

'I'm heading out that way,' Tosh said, pointing east. 'Looks flatter than any other direction.'

'I'm going to stretch my legs and then I'll join Mary on these calculations,' said Anna.

Tosh had already set off across the plain and I followed, watching him weave his way through the rocks, gradually catching up with him.

'Why does the Martian surface have so many scattered rocks covering it?' he asked.

'Amazing as it might seem,' I said, 'many of these rocks were carried along by ice and dumped here when the ice melted. A long time ago, of course.'

'The rocks aren't from around here?'

'Probably not, but I don't have the equipment to check.' I stooped to pick up a pineapple-sized boulder, and examine it. 'Hmm, this is basalt, so possibly just brought here by wind.'

'Surely the wind isn't strong enough for that?' Tosh said in surprise.

'If it is that, then it is a slow process. Note how most of the rocks have a build-up of dust behind them on the western side.'

'But the prevailing wind here is from the east.'

'Yes,' I said. 'The rocks move towards the wind.'

'How is that possible?'

'The wind blows away the dust on the east side of the stones. Eventually a hollow is created and the rock slips into it. The pile of dust on the west side is then blown away and starts to build up against the stone once more. It is a really slow process. That might be the mechanism here or the alternative is the rocks being carried on ice. Probably the latter here as with wind effects the stones tend to be more evenly spaced.'

'I had no idea. Look at this,' said Tosh, kicking into the surface. 'It's a dust-filled crater. We need to avoid these when the tank touches down. But where is the crater rim?'

'Worn away over millennia. This was almost certainly a lake bed at some time in the past. I'd need to read up on the papers written about it.'

We trudged onwards. Tosh stopped and began to kick away the dust from underfoot. 'This is good. Solid bedrock. Now, let's check how large this area is.'

'Yes, basalt. Perfect,' I said.

Thirty minutes later, we'd established that the solid basalt here spread at least fifty metres in each direction and was covered with no more than a few centimetres of regolith, which would be blown away by the exhaust from the tank's landing jets. By eye, it looked pretty flat too. Tosh walked to the centre of the area.

'Chi, do you copy?' said Tosh.

'Copy you,' said Chi.

'Mark my position.'

'Marked,' Chi said.

'You have at least fifty metres diameter from here of solid basalt covered with light regolith,' Tosh said.

'Brilliant,' said Chi. 'I'll program in the coordinates.'

'Copy that,' said Tosh, 'but you mustn't miss that spot as there are old hidden craters containing regolith dotted around the plain.'

'Copy that,' said Chi. 'Let me know if you find anything to make it even more complicated!'

Tosh laughed. 'See you soon,' he said.

'Never fear,' she replied.

'Can't believe we're on Mars,' I said.

'No. Amazing.'

In the far east a range of low hills, actually called the East Hills, spread softly across the horizon. Not huge, not jagged, just gentle and undulating. Between us and them, the rock-strewn plain was the floor of Gusev crater. So littered with rocks was it that, when walking, great care had to be taken not to trip and fall. The whole scene was a rusty brownish red colour.

Looking back to the west, there was hardly any raised ground in view, but hills far beyond the horizon were doing their best to peek across the extensive width of

Gusev. In the near distance, about eight hundred metres away, the Rimor sat alone, looking for all the world like a child's toy or some museum diorama.

'Let's get back, Tosh. We don't want to be near here when the tank arrives.'

We walked back towards the Rimor, me occasionally hanging back to collect rocks and place them into a bag I had strung on my waist.

∞∞∞∞∞∞∞∞∞∞∞∞

'That's the tank separated,' said Chi. 'We have a four-minute hold before we start the descent.'

'Copy that, Chi,' I said. 'Let us know when you're at ten thousand metres. We're all outside.'

'Copy that, Mark.'

Forty minutes later, Chi gave us the heads-up and we all scoured the eastern sky. What a sight. The tank, trailed by a spluttering cloud of smoke and heat tiles, could just be seen high in the southeast.

'Five thousand metres,' said Chi.

'Copy that,' said Anna.

The trail had disappeared and the tank was now a distinctly elongated shape heading towards the surface. Now descending tail first, its orange colour became clear and the exhaust from the engines could be seen as it fought the higher speed winds in the upper atmosphere.

'Two thousand metres,' said Chi.

'Copy that,' I said. 'We have eyeballs on it. Wonderful sight. Mary's filming it.'

'Copy that,' said Chi.

111

The cylinder was now clearly visible as it dropped through a thousand metres to five hundred and slowed still further as it approached our designated landing site. Automatic systems opened the legs ready for touchdown.

'Nearly there, Chi,' I said.

'Copy that, fifty metres,' said Chi.

The landing legs were now fully extended as the huge tank reached the ground. Billowing dust clouds almost obscured it; the top of the tank was the only part visible.

'Touch down,' said Chi.

'Copy that,' said Anna. 'Magnificent to watch. Swallowed by dust clouds as yet.'

The regolith gradually returned to the surface of Mars and the tank stood solidly on its basalt plinth.

'Let's go and check everything is okay,' I said and the four of us made our way across the stony plain.

Anna was the first to arrive. 'Four degrees off vertical,' she said.

'On it,' said Tosh, using the pneumatics to crank up the northerly leg.

Small adjustments had to be made to the eastern and western legs until Anna announced, 'Zero degrees.'

'Okay,' I said. 'Tosh, can you detach the tethers. They won't be needed. We'll be leaving as soon as we're all on board.'

I watched as the tethers fell from the hub on the top of the tank and coiled like a tangled hose on the regolith.

Thirty minutes later, we were inside the Rimor, removing our pressure suits, donning our flight suits, and preparing to depart.

'What's our departure window?' asked Anna.

'Not for eighteen minutes. Better twenty-five minutes,' said Chi.

'Rimor, Spirit, Neil here,' said the radio. 'I don't think it will arrive in time to bother you guys, but the orbiter is showing a dust storm coming from the east. We estimate that you have an hour, minimum, out.'

'Can you see it, Chi?' asked Anna.

'Yes. Don't think there is much wind speed involved. It's well clear of you,' said Chi.

We sat in our couches, hoping that there would be no complications in docking with the tank.

'Five minutes to docking manoeuvre,' said Anna.

'Copy that,' said Chi.

∞∞∞∞∞∞∞∞∞∞

I felt the jets activate and Anna lifted off, guiding us towards the tank. In the far distance beyond it, the horizon and East Hills were blurred with the dust being carried by the storm. As we approached the tank, Anna changed us into the vertical position and activated the automatic docking program.

'Fuel four per cent,' said the computer.

Maintaining a hovering vertical position was always fuel intensive. I heard a clunk from beneath my feet.

'Docking brackets locked,' said the computer. Then after about fifteen seconds it added, 'Fuel hoses connected.'

'Engines off,' said Anna. 'Computer, begin pumping fuel.'

'Pumping commencing.'

My stress levels were rising. I couldn't take my eyes off the indication of the tank's vertical alignment. We stood by for the confirmation of the tanks being full.

'Rimor hydrogen tank now at one hundred per cent. Oxygen tank at ninety-five per cent.' said the computer. A few seconds later it confirmed both tanks were full.

'Computer, disconnect hoses,' said Anna. 'Prepare for lift-off. Chi, confirm you are ready.'

'Hoses disconnected,' said the computer.

'Copy that. You have a go,' said Chi.

'Five, four, three, two, ignition,' said Anna.

The Rimor shook as its engines joined with those of the tank to provide the thrust to take us into orbit.

'Lift-off,' said Anna.

With the low gravity on Mars, the vibration and noise were less noticeable than it was on Earth, but the sense of the power being generated by the engines was palpable.

'Two thousand metres. Stable,' said the computer.

From the cockpit windows, we could see the ground rapidly falling away.

'Ten thousand metres. Stable.'

The curvature of the planet was now becoming clear to us and the dust storm was visible to the east.

The computer continued to call altitude as the trajectory changed ready for undocking.

'Prepare for separation,' said Anna.

All of a sudden, the craft was in silence. Sounds from outside told us the mechanics of undocking had been completed. The falling sensation was replaced by more acceleration as the Rimor, alone now, climbed towards its rendezvous with Spirit and the tank fell back to leave yet more human debris on the planet's surface.

Freefall! The main engines had completed their task.

'MECO[4],' said Anna. 'Fuel level, please, computer.'

'Fuel eighteen per cent, Anna.'

Plenty for manoeuvring in orbit.

'Have visual on you,' said Chi.

'Copy that, Chi. KURS locked on,' said Anna. KURS was the computer system which would automatically dock us to Spirit.

'Copy that, Anna,' said Chi.

Forty minutes later, the docking clamps rattled our hull as we connected to Spirit. Anna climbed into the docking tunnel to check seals from our end, but most of the checks were taking place on Spirit's side of the tunnel where Bill would be securing each clamp individually. It was a time consuming process, but essential. If a seal broke, we would all be very dead, very quickly.

Relief surged through me as we transferred to the spacious interior of Spirit, where we could get a more thorough wash and change of clothing.

---

[4] MECO – Main Engine Cut Off

14 Home Again

It was wonderful to be back at home with Linda and Jason.

It hadn't been instant, though. We were held in quarantine on board Spirit for twenty-eight days. Then a team of astronauts, specially flown up to Spirit to carry out the task, began disinfecting and cleaning every area we had used on Spirit and the Rimor which had descended to the surface.

Fortunately, their first task had been to disinfect us. Once that was done, we could return to Earth and leave them to finish the job and seal the samples into airtight containers and transfer them to Earth for examination in a secure section at the Johnson Space Center.

I had just a few days undisturbed with my family before beginning a schedule clogged with interviews and television appearances. Mary, the first human on Mars, was most in demand and it became a problem for her as she had an enormous workload to prepare for the main event – our expedition to Trappist-1.

The Rimor we'd used to land on Mars no longer had heat tiles, so once it had been given the all-clear by the quarantine team, it became a permanent addition to the ISS. A brand new Rimor was launched to join to Spirit. Two fully laden tanks were also launched and attached. An additional fuel supply came from the moon to top up the third tank attached to Spirit. For the Mars expedition, the tanks had only contained roughly fifty per cent of the fuel which we'd need to lift off from the most massive Trappist-1 worlds.

Eventually, SpaceX told us, they were planning an orbital dry dock where the Rimor could be taken inside a larger station and new tiles fitted, but that was still a few years away.

We were all excited and anticipation was beginning to grow. A British EBC film crew arrived at the Johnson Space Center to interview the six of us prior to our departure. I was surprised to find they had changed from being the British Broadcasting Corporation to the English Broadcasting Corporation. 'What was that all about?' I asked, but my question just received blank stares from the crew who were in a hurry to get started.

'Dr Noble, you are the commander of the expedition. Is everyone prepared?'

'Yes,' I said. 'We've been training for almost a year now and think we have most eventualities covered.'

'Are you expecting to find life?'

'I'll let Dr MacIntosh answer that,' I said.

Tosh cleared his throat and took a sip of water. 'That is the great unknown, of course, but several of the Trappist-1 worlds hold promise.'

'Why is that?'

'Water. We are fairly certain that D, E and F have liquid water on the surface. Now whether that is the odd lake, an ice sheet or extensive oceans, we can't possibly know. That's the reason for the trip.'

'And water means life?'

'Well,' said Tosh, 'It certainly adds to the possibility. We think water is a crucial ingredient in the processes which create life as we understand it.'

'Sounds like Spock saying, "life as we know it".'

Tosh laughed. 'Yes, I suppose it does and it is meant in that way. Other life forms might not require water. Perhaps a silicon life form. However, for the sort of life we have on Earth, water is crucial.'

'Could there be intelligent life?'

'Any life would be fascinating, whether it be plant or microbes. Mars has been such a disappointment so far. There was no sign of life anywhere we visited on the Mars mission, even in the deep riverbed cores,' said Tosh. 'Frankly, whatever we find will be fascinating. Sophisticated life would be a bonus, really.'

'Dr Carter, as well as being the first human to set foot on an alien planet, you also invented this spolding flight system. How does it work?'

Mary replied, 'There have been many documentaries about the methodology, and I'd direct interested parties there. Simply, we reach into the hidden, dark-matter universe, pluck our destination, bring it to us, swivel into hyperspace, and allow it to take us with it as it returns to where it was in normal space time.'

'How did it feel to be the first to set foot on another world? You famously said, "Apollo might have represented a giant leap for mankind, but this is a stepping stone to the rest of the universe!" I suppose you thought long and hard about it.'

'No, I didn't actually.' Mary laughed. 'I didn't realise I was to be first until I was standing on the ladder. I had only twenty seconds or so to come up with something. Also, we must not forget that the moon is "another world" too,' Mary said severely. 'I was the first to set foot on Mars, a second world. Neil Armstrong and Buzz Aldrin were the real explorers. They were first to land on and stand somewhere other than Earth. I was flattered to be chosen to be first on Mars, but it is no big deal compared with their achievement.'

'I think you are being very modest.'

'I disagree,' said Mary. 'We are about to enter a new era of exploration. Within a decade, we might have set foot on dozens of new worlds. Being first on Mars is an insignificant achievement, and being blown out of all proportion.'

Each of us received similar questions and I think we were all relieved when it was over and we were able to relax with the television crew and enjoy a few glasses of wine. Less dramatic and more personal questions could then pass to and fro. I still didn't get any answers on the television company's name change.

The EBC item encouraged the media to clamour for more interviews and the last one was with me alone, shortly before we left on that first interstellar voyage.

'What are you expecting to find?' asked the presenter from CNN.

'If we knew that,' I said, 'we wouldn't need to go.'

'Yes, but you must have some hopes and expectations.'

'We hope that we will find one of the planets to be habitable. Trappist-1's D, E, and F worlds hold the most potential, but we shouldn't be disappointed if they are all dead worlds. The expedition will give us experience landing and taking off from a world far larger than our moon or Mars. Apart from D, which is smaller, they are all close to the size and mass of the Earth. We'll learn a huge amount.'

'Do you think you'll find life?'

'Hopefully, but these dwarf sun planetary systems have a lot going against them for life, as well as some positives.'

'What are the positives?'

'Several are in the Goldilocks zone and might have liquid water. Our type of life needs water to exist,' I said.

'And against?'

'The planets could be tidally locked which could—'

'Tidally locked?'

'It means they could have one face permanently facing their sun, like the way the moon faces Earth, particularly as this planetary system might be twice the age of the solar system. A tidally locked planet is likely to have one side frozen and the other side extremely hot. Life would then only be possible in the twilight zones, and such a planet might have raging winds whipping around the entire globe. Not good for life getting a foothold, and it could make it impossible to use our landing system. Wind speed is critical.'

'So, when you say "habitable", you don't mean you are expecting life to already be there?'

'No. Not necessarily, but the planet might be somewhere humankind could live. That is what we want to know. Humans are a colonising species – if we find a planet we could build a colony upon, you can be certain there would be people who would want to settle it.'

The interview lasted another twenty minutes and then I was freed to plan our departure.

∞∞∞∞∞∞∞∞∞∞

Another farewell to Linda and Jason and we were soon in orbit. Spirit was moving to a safe distance ready for the journey to Trappist-1. The expedition was only supposed to last a month or thereabouts but was packed with enough emergency dried food and water to last more than a year. A month would be enough time to survey the most interesting planets and to make a planetary landing on the best. I wouldn't be back before Easter, but it shouldn't be much later than May or June.

Eventually, Spirit was in position. The spolding device was pinpointing Trappist-1E. Mary made more delicate adjustments then told us we were ready to go.

Our computer took over, creating the slow rotation to face our axis along the line which would take us from Earth to a world in another solar system.

'Holding at five seconds,' said Anna.

A few seconds later, mission control said, 'You have a go to complete countdown.'

'Thank you, NASA,' I said.

Anna said, 'Ready, five, four, three, two, one, zero!'

15 Hyperspace Again

We thought we knew what to expect this time. The warning of being crushed or killed by shock no longer worried us. The Mars trip had seemed to last no more than a few seconds although Mary had been quite concerned that it lasted any time at all. She really thought it would have been instantaneous and had a team of astrophysicists trying to understand why it wasn't.

Yet again, I found myself feeling as if I was glued to my couch. I couldn't move my arms and it wasn't owing to gravity, but something in the very environment of the ship. Again the air seemed to have congealed around our bodies. It immobilised me. I was rigidly fixed in position.

I tried to turn my head to see Mary. My head wouldn't rotate. My entity managed to swivel my eyes left for me, I could see Mary's hands as stationary as mine and the same with Anna to my right. Could I breathe?

I attempted to inhale – my chest rose, air flooded inwards, but again I think it was with help from my entity. I exhaled. Yes, I could breathe. I felt my heart pounding but it was nothing I hadn't experienced during hard physical labour or at the gym. *Why hadn't it ended?* At least a minute had passed according to the dashboard clock. Its electronics seemed unaffected by the stasis.

What was outside?

The windows no longer showed stars, or the moon which had been hanging in the top right of my vision when the countdown started. There was a greenish tint to the blackness of space. No flashing lights or sense of movement could be felt. To all intents and purposes, we seemed to be absolutely stationary, yet I could hear the nuclear generator whining under full power. *That meant time must be passing, surely? Could a sound continue if time weren't progressing? Wouldn't sound cease if time did too?* Anyway, the clock was definitely progressing. It passed two minutes.

I was still gripped by the irresistible force. How much time had passed? Three minutes. One scientist had said that our journey would be proportional to the actual time light took to move between our departure and arrival points. Mars was just ten light minutes from Earth and we were locked in position for a few seconds, maybe five seconds. Trappist-1 was forty light years away. I let my entity help with the mental calculation. If it were five seconds for ten light minutes, how long would it be for forty light years?

In a few seconds we had calculated the proportionate time. My God! It was one hundred and twenty days. Four months! Would I be sitting here for four months? Unable to move. Dehydration would kill me in a few days. Had Mary sentenced us all to a horrible death, staring at this greenish-black hyperspace until our bodies ceased to function? Would six decomposed corpses arrive at Trappist-1, to one day be discovered and be puzzled over by other interstellar travellers? My mouth dried at the thought of dehydration and I put a huge effort into raising the index finger of my right hand.

Nothing. It didn't even tremble. Movement was absolutely impossible. I tried to say, 'Anna', but my lips wouldn't move and all I heard myself emit was a muffled moan. I took another breath. At least we weren't going to suffocate, although death might have come quicker that way.

How much time had passed? The dashboard clock said we'd been in our frozen state for nearly an hour now. Panic started to set in. *How many days could I survive without water?* My entity told me it would normally be three days, but, with his help, it could be extended to a week.

What a horrible death. My fellow astronauts were within touching distance, but we were unable to communicate or assist each other. When the dash clock said ninety minutes, I'd run out of ideas. Spolding had sentenced us all to a horrible death.

All of a sudden the whole ship vibrated and our torture ended. We were thrown forward violently and I heard grunts and gasps from my crewmates. We were in freefall again, the straps holding us to our seats to prevent us floating away. How long had it been? The clock on my screen read 1:36:13. Just over ninety-six minutes. It is amazing the horror which can go through your mind in such a short period of time. Thank God it was all over. My shoulders sagged with relief. I looked at the windows.

Stars.

I dimmed the bridge lights. The stars looked no different to how they did at home. In fact, the constellation of Orion was blazing directly in front of us. Maybe we hadn't left Earth. Where were Trappist-1 and its planets?

'Phew,' said Bill from behind me. 'That was, well… different.'

'Yes,' said Mary. 'Like being held in stasis. Was beginning to feel as if we might be locked up for forty years.'

'Yes, me too,' said Tosh.

'I think we're all in the *me too* club,' I said. 'I did not like that at all!'

'My entity is most unhappy,' said Anna. 'Tells me she didn't like the feeling of constriction.'

'No. Mine neither,' said Chi, reaching back to make contact with Tosh's hand.

'Where's the star?' mumbled Tosh, fiddling with controls on his science station, a cluster of instruments to one side of his couch. 'And where's the planet, come to that? Checking for radiation.'

'Don't know,' said Anna. 'I'll rotate us.'

The Orion constellation drifted off to the right and, all of a sudden, red light flooded the bridge. The red dwarf star, Trappist-1 appeared slightly smaller than the sun from Earth. It was indeed distinctly red, and too bright to look at directly.

'Radiation nominal,' said Tosh. 'Similar to being outside on the moon. For God's sake, where's the planet, Anna?'

'Patience, Tosh,' Anna said, and continued the rotation.

'We're at another sun,' said Bill. 'How amazing is that? We're the first people ever to visit another solar system.'

'Yes, cool,' I said, my skin tingling with excitement.

Trappist-1 continued to drift across our field of vision, disappearing into the wings and allowing us to see the stars again as well as a pale disc, a tenth the size of the moon, right of centre stage.

'Is that it?' asked Tosh.

'No. That's its neighbour – planet F,' said Anna, pointing at the misty crescent world.

We turned full circle and Orion reappeared. Planet E must be above or below us.

Our rotation stopped.

'Rotating through ninety degrees upwards,' said Anna.

We'd barely begun to rotate upwards when the stars were swallowed by an impenetrable darkness. Something was eating the heavens, at least from our perspective but, peering at the dark circle emerging above us, I could see a haze of light at its edge. We'd arrived exactly where we'd intended. Trappist-1E was gradually introducing itself to us. The last part to appear was illuminated. Most of what we were seeing was the nightside of the world.

'Wow!' said Mary.

'Double wow!' came from Anna.

'Can you stop the movement, Anna?' I asked. 'Give us a chance to take this in.'

'Yes, a second,' said Anna, and I felt some thrusters slowing our spin and leaving us pointing directly towards the alien world.

'When do we see the daylight side?' I asked.

'We're descending,' said Anna. 'I'm going to adjust our speed to put us into a high orbit.'

'What's our altitude?' asked Mary.

'Thirty thousand miles,' said Anna. 'Almost geosynchronous, so if I do nothing we'll stay fixed above the same spot on the surface.'

'Is the planet rotating?' asked Bill.

'Yes,' said Mary, looking at her computer displays. 'It's not tidally locked. Nice surprise. Probably the influence of its neighbours.'

I asked, 'Can you take us down to a couple of hundred miles, Mary, to give us a chance to see more of the surface.'

'Just checking the depth of atmosphere first, Mark,' Anna said. We needed to be sure that Spirit remained outside of any atmosphere or its orbit would quickly deteriorate. 'Atmosphere seems to be about three hundred and twenty miles, so similar to but a little greater than Earth. I'll take us into an orbit just under four hundred miles. How's radiation, Tosh? Any Van Allen belts?'

'Yes. It does have a magnetic field,' said Tosh. 'Stronger than Earth's so we know it has a liquid core. There are Van Allen belts, so get us through them as quickly as possible for the sake of our entities, please, Anna.'

'Okay, taking us in,' she said, and I felt a strong deceleration. It was threatening to throw me forward out of my seat and I tightened my straps to keep me secure.

I kept looking towards the planet's horizon where the daylight side was getting closer but actually moving away with the rotation of the planet. Soon we were looking solely at the jet black disc of E's night side.

'Oh, did you see that?' asked Bill.

'What?' asked Chi.

'Lightning flash. Oh. There's another and another. Over to the right,' said Bill excitedly.

The planet was celebrating our arrival with fireworks – a truly impressive electrical storm. The more I looked, the more lightning I saw.

'They've got weather, then,' said Tosh.

'Clouds too,' Chi said, as more sheet lightening flickered in the cloudy heavens over to our starboard side.

The ship's acceleration ceased. Anna said, 'Altitude three hundred and seventy-five miles. Stabilising the orbit.'

'Copy that,' Chi said.

'We've got water vapour, oxygen and nitrogen,' said Tosh. 'A bit heavy with carbon dioxide but possibly breathable.'

'Any harmful trace gases?' I asked.

'Some ozone and methane, which is promising,' Tosh said.

'The signatures of life,' said Bill quietly.

'Fingers crossed,' I said back to him.

The daylight on the left had now vanished. The entire disc was black, then, almost imperceptibly, the tiniest sliver of brightness appeared on the right. The rotation of the planet had finally caught up with our orbital manoeuvres and day was dawning on the new world.

16 E

Our eyes all turned towards the emerging daylight. Initially it was nothing but a bluish haze along that limb of the planet, but soon, the twilit surface became visible. Shapes of land masses and seas. There was liquid water and swirling clouds. It looked so much like Earth, yet something wasn't quite right.

As we travelled towards the day, the blue seas sparkled and the higher land was covered with snow, appearing pale pink in Trappist-1's dawn rays. There was snow even in the equatorial region, but these were not mountains as we knew them on Earth, more like very high hills. Yet something odd greeted our senses.

Cloud patterns were familiar, creating the shapes which followed the same high and low pressure we witnessed in our own skies, but something was certainly wrong with the scene.

There was no green. We could see grey and brown and even black areas, but no forests, grasslands or jungles. Could the entire world be dead? Yet it looked as if it could be so alive. It had water in abundance and an atmosphere which might even be breathable by us. *Had life never evolved here? Had planet E been waiting all these billions of years for humankind to arrive and settle it?* A virgin world, untouched by cellular life.

'It's dead,' said Tosh. 'Just rock and water. Nothing growing. Nothing living.'

'Well, we don't know that, Tosh,' said Chi. 'The seas could be teeming with life.'

'Perhaps,' Tosh said sullenly.

I supposed we all had our own hopes and wishes about planet E, but what we saw beneath us gave no indication of life.

We undid our straps and floated free of our couches, pulling ourselves over to the windows which revealed a growing vista of a truly alien planet.

'A lot of black around the shorelines and lower hills. Wonder if it is a type of rock,' I said.

'Could be plant life,' said Tosh. 'To get the most out of the red light from Trappist-1, plants could be more black than green to absorb the sun's rays.'

'Hmm, yes,' I said. 'Hadn't thought about that. Maybe there's life after all. Okay, stay or no stay.'

'Stay,' Mary, Anna and Chi piped up simultaneously.

'Right. Mary, check what you can see of Sol on the targeting device. Make sure we have our return route sorted,' I said.

Mary busied herself with her instruments. 'Point us towards these coordinates.'

Chi strapped herself back into her couch and warned us all that there would be some gentle vectors. We all held on to something close to where we were floating.

Despite the rotation being extremely slow, it was difficult not to be pulled into each other against one wall. As soon as it stopped, we all returned to our couches and lightly strapped ourselves in.

A few more vectors moved Spirit backwards and forwards, side to side, until Chi said, 'That's your coordinates, Mary.'

Mary peered at her screen and I leaned over to watch. 'That's Sol,' she said, as a bright star came to the centre of her display.

'Hard to believe that it is still the twentieth century there. 1991,' Bill said, wistfully.

'Shame we can't signal some sports bets!' said Tosh.

Mary zoomed in. I watched it becoming brighter, then developing a distinct disc. Once it filled the screen, Mary began searching the blackness nearby.

It took nearly forty minutes for her to finally find a planet. 'Bingo,' she said. 'That's Jupiter.'

'We need Earth,' I said.

'No, actually we don't. We can get back to the solar system via Jupiter. This will do for now,' said Mary.

'Let's find a landing site then,' said Tosh. 'I want to secure my immortality by setting foot on this place.'

Chi set Mary's coordinates then turned us back towards planet E. Most of us grabbed binoculars and, filled with excitement, started to study the rotating landscape beneath, but Tosh concentrated on his instruments.

'Strong winds on the equator,' he said.

'How strong?' I asked.

'Gusts of at least forty miles per hour. Not healthy for landing the tanks.'

'SpaceX said the maximum should be under fifteen with gusts of no more than twenty, so that won't do, even with the new extended legs,' said Chi.

'Okay,' said Tosh. 'Looking at the tropics. More snow there, so less exposed ground.'

'I think the black stuff is plants,' said Bill. 'It seems to be thicker at the coastline and more sparse as the distance to the sea opens.'

'Definitely no radio or other electronic signatures,' said Anna.

'So any life other than the plants is primitive or non-existent?' I asked.

'Looks like it,' agreed Anna.

'Guys,' said Tosh 'That flat area to the north of the elongated island has winds under five miles per hour. It's in the lee of the hills which run the length of the island. Let's monitor that for an E day. Could be a good spot to set down.'

We used our telescopic cameras to take close-up shots of the island. It was around sixty miles long and twelve wide, shaped a little like Madagascar. A range of hills ran its length, higher in the north, reaching about one thousand metres and lower in the south. At the northwest end the hills pushed to the east coast, leaving a large area, maybe six or seven miles square, almost flat. Its fringes were covered with the same black plant-like material. High powered lenses showed that as the vegetation reached any ground over about twenty metres, it thinned out. Whether that was the cold or some other reason wasn't clear. Maybe it needed to receive spray from the oceans to survive. Was it a seaweed, making an excursion onto land as had once happened on the primitive Earth?

'What sort of temperatures will we be exposed to down there?' I asked.

'Land is reading ten centigrade. The sea a fraction higher,' said Tosh.

'Will we continue to pass over this area, Chi?' I asked.

'Roughly,' she said. 'Our orbit is twenty degrees off the equator. Might not see it if we're at the southern end of our orbit, but it will be visible every other orbit.'

'What's the length of our orbit?' I asked.

'One hundred minutes,' Chi replied.

'What's the day, down there, Tosh?' Anna asked.

'Just over thirty hours,' he replied.

'Okay,' I said as I came to my decision. 'Let's monitor that location for ten orbits, build up a weather pattern and if it is all within safety parameters, we'll send down a tank. How does that sound?'

There were nods and murmurs of approval.

17 Haven

After a sleep period, I floated back into the cockpit. The planet was in night, so I dimmed the lights and looked at the vibrant star fields which surrounded us. There was Sol, comfortingly bright but not the brightest in the sky. It was nothing special to look at, yet was home to humankind. A fragile environment.

Dawn broke over the far limb of Haven, the name we had given planet E.

'Ah, this is where you're hiding,' said Tosh, pulling himself alongside me.

'Beautiful,' I said, euphoric at the vista before me.

'Sure is.'

'You looked at the landing site data?' I asked.

'Came in to do just that,' he said and pushed off towards his couch.

'Maximum wind in the last thirty hours has been seven miles per hour. Was under one mile per hour most of that period each time it was within range of my instruments. Day temperatures were as low as four and reached a maximum of eleven centigrade. We'll need overcoats,' he said and laughed.

'Remarkably temperate,' I said.

'Yes. It'll be better than working at minus fifty which is what the astronomers told us would be likely on planet E.'

'Do you think the black stuff is really plant life?'

'Yes, Mark. The growth pattern is pretty conclusive. Seaweed, which can also live on land near the water too, most likely. Either high humidity feeds the on-land plant or it uses capillaries to move the water from the nearest source.'

'Wonder if there is more life in the oceans,' I said.

'Well, the sooner we get down there, the sooner we'll find out. Who are you taking this time?'

'You, Bill and Chi,' I said. 'I want Bill to help manhandle equipment with you or me.'

'Chi will be pleased,' he said.

'You don't have to hide your relationship, you know.'

'Well, I don't approve of work and romance conflicting.'

'Serious, is it?'

'Enough that we're thinking of tying the knot when we get back.'

'Linda and I managed fine enough. Doesn't need to affect work,' I said.

'I know, but I'm still a bit old-school. Keep quiet about it. Chi might not like to think you knew.'

'The hand-holding is a bit of a giveaway!' I said and laughed.

∞∞∞∞∞∞∞∞∞∞∞

Anna sat at the controls of Rimor. Chi and I watched as she armed the switches for separation from tank lander number one.

'Armed and ready,' she said.

'Okay, go for separation,' I said.

We heard a mechanical clunk from beneath us and the huge tank, packed full of propellant, drifted away.

'Rotating,' said Anna.

'Copy,' said Chi as the tank swivelled and came back into view in front of the cockpit, turning to be ninety degrees to Spirit.

Controlling it remotely, Anna turned it so that it faced rear-end to our direction of travel. More thrusters caused it to move away from us until it reached a safe distance.

'Looking good,' said Chi.

'Safe distance,' confirmed Anna. 'Mary, we're oriented for descent. Just give me a go when we're in the right location.'

'Roger that, Anna,' said Mary over the intercom. 'Around twelve minutes. I'll give you a "mark" at one.'

'Copy that,' said Anna.

The bright orange tank, looking even more red than normal in the rays of Trappist-1, hung in space before us with the planet beyond, the daylight dividing line moving to the left.

'Get ready,' said Mary. 'Five, four, three, two, one, *mark*!'

Anna snapped a switch. 'Countdown running,' she said.

Chi said, 'Ten seconds.'

She counted down to zero and Anna pressed the "FIRE" button on her panel. A haze appeared at the tail of the tank and it moved away from us, relentlessly gaining speed as it began the precarious descent into Haven's atmosphere.

As we lost sight of it, we studied the two monitors. There was more vibration than we'd encountered on the Mars mission.

Once the braking manoeuvre was over, the tank was turned so that it was heading nose first into the atmosphere. The flanges were open protecting the larger landing legs from the gathering heat. Out of our sight, the inflatable heat shield will have opened to protect the top of the tank. We could clearly see the glow of the heat during the descent.

'Entering blackout,' said Anna.

The video images disappeared, unable to be transmitted through the ionisation which hugged the craft like a corona.

'Six minutes,' said Anna.

So frustrating, not being able to see what is going right, or worse, wrong.

'Ten minutes,' said Anna.

'Fifteen minutes,' said Anna.

Haven had a marginally thicker atmosphere than Earth. All we could do was hope for the best.

Images reappeared on the monitor, showing the flanges had done their job. The tank was still heading nose forward, so we were, as yet, not seeing the surface.

'More forceful jet stream than Mars,' said Anna.

'Still stable. Within tolerances. We'll be through it soon,' said Chi.

'Inflatable heatshield gone,' said Anna. 'Auto rotation any moment.'

The monitors showed the huge tank swivelling until we saw the land beneath the flanges.

'Ready for sloughing,' said Anna.

The flanges dramatically broke away, taking many of the tiles with them.

'Five thousand metres,' said Chi.

'On target,' said Anna.

The tank was now in wispy low cloud, as its motors fired to maintain its vertical orientation. Then the cloud cover broke.

'Two thousand metres,' said Chi.

Now we could see the landing site, the flat plain and shoreline.

'Hundred metres. Spot on target!' said Chi. 'Fifty metres. Legs deploying.'

'*Touchdown!*' said Anna. 'Motor shutdown. Standing vertical. Sensors read wind at six miles per hour.'

The dust or sand thrown up on landing slowly cleared with the motors now off. We were on the ground. The heat seemed to have vaporised the black material as it cleared its own landing area of the strange plant-like carpet.

The tank had landed on a planet circling another star! The monitors showed us very little, just the landing area and scorched rock. At the fringes was the alien plant life.

'Completely stable,' said Anna. 'Nought point one per cent off vertical. Couldn't be more perfect.'

The monitor showed a cable falling from the top of the tank then coiling loosely beside the legs.

'That's the tethers released,' said Chi.

The left monitor swivelled and we could take in the scene looking towards the sea.

Bill, Tosh and Mary were now looking over our shoulders. The camera stilled, rotated through ninety degrees and the vista swivelled to horizontal.

'Wow!' said Mary.

The plain was certainly flat. In the foreground we saw some small boulders, a larger one in the middle distance. The black substance covered everything in that direction, right down to the water. Gentle waves approached the beach, hardly breaking and running up the shoreline. The sea was dark and oily in appearance, complementing the vegetation.

'Atmospheric pressure about ten per cent greater than Earth,' said Tosh. 'Temperature a cool five C.'

Chi swivelled the camera to look inland.

Beyond the edge of the incinerated circle the plants continued into the distance, where spurs from eroded low hills pointed accusing fingers towards the ocean.

As the land climbed, the plant life became thinner until nothing but bare rock could be seen. Far away, the hills were crested in white, or what passed for white under the red rays of Trappist-1. No shrubs, bushes, trees or any other sign of Earth-like vegetation, nor animal life, but to be fair, animals would likely have been scared away by the tank's landing engines. Did it mean that this world had evolved just one plant which dominated. Was there other life? Insects, small animals or other creatures not being seen by our cameras? Was the ocean teeming with life as it was on Earth? The cradle of evolution, but with creatures which never ventured out onto the continents. A water world, perchance?

There was only one way to find out.

'First excursion, Tosh, Bill, Chi and me,' I said. 'I need Bill, for his pure physical strength and Tosh because he is also a biologist as well as being a medical doctor. We need to concentrate on finding life.'

We continued to monitor the screens as Chi swivelled and zoomed the two cameras.

I supposed that if there was any way for an alien world to be boring, this would be a prime example. Blacks and browns dominated the scene.

18 Descent

The Rimor was ready. We had enough stores for a couple of weeks plus backup emergency supplies. The cupboards were filled with scientific equipment, containers, microscopes and many electronic sensors and scanners. Unlike the Mars trip, we were also carrying an inflatable boat and a submersible. As Haven had an Earth-like atmospheric pressure, the full-pressure suits were securely stowed. The simple airtight suits would be sufficient for this expedition. Hopefully, we'd be able to breathe the air and discard the backpacks.

Chi occupied the pilot's seat, with me in the command slot. Behind us were Tosh and Bill. Chi's pink and yellow mouse-faced childhood cuddly toy sat on top of the dashboard – her mascot. It was called Shooey and she tapped it for good fortune. It smiled back at us, indifferent to our hopes and fears.

'Separating,' said Chi.

We heard the undocking noises and through the windows we could see that we were drifting away from Spirit.

Chi applied some gentle thrust to take us to a safe distance.

'Two thousand metres,' said Chi. 'Orientating.'

'Three, two, one, mark!' said Mary over the radio.

Chi hit the automatic countdown. Once again we were waiting. In one minute we'd be on our way to the surface.

'Zero,' announced Chi and we felt the main engines start. They fired for twenty-five seconds, slowing us down and causing us to enter Haven's atmosphere.

Once the engines cut off, Chi swung us around and that put the hull in the correct position for atmospheric entry. The Rimor began to vibrate as the hull bit into the fringes of the atmosphere.

The flames and sparks were far more noticeable as we pierced the heavier air of Haven. Outside, the heat shield was gradually vaporising. By the time we were through the worst, only the lightweight polymer-aluminium skin would remain… as long as SpaceX had got it right!

Once through the dangers of entry into the atmosphere, the Rimor became a sophisticated glider, Chi working the flight surfaces to control our angle of descent.

'Twenty thousand metres,' said the computer.

Radio blackout was over. 'Spirit, Rimor here, do you copy? Over,' said Chi.

'Copy you,' replied Mary. 'Any problems?'

'No, excellent, gradually slowing.'

We descended rapidly towards the land mass we recognised from orbit.

'Under Mach 1,' said Chi.

To the north of the continent was our landing site on the island we'd christened, New Manhattan.

'Five thousand metres,' said Chi. 'New Manhattan visible.'

'Hey, I can see the tank,' said Bill from behind me.

The orange structure stood out against the blacks, greys and browns of the landscape below.

'Powering up,' said Chi, and we all waited with anticipation to sense the engines coming into play.

'Under power,' said Chi.

'Copy that,' said Mary from orbit.

The Rimor was now behaving exactly as it had on Mars and during tests on Earth. Chi's expert hands had it under control as it made its way towards the tank.

Chi banked us around the landing area, giving us excellent views of the sea and adjacent headlands.

'Happy with that location in front of us?' asked Chi.

'Looks good,' I said. 'Tosh?'

'Keep clear of the plants, as that could mark highwater point,' Tosh said.

'No problem,' said Chi, swinging the aircraft around so that it pointed towards the tank. The nose lifted and we came to a halt, maybe ten metres above the ground, a hundred and fifty metres from the tank. Chi eased off the power and we settled gently onto a plant-free area thirty metres from the water.

'Engines cut,' said Chi.

'Copy that,' said Mary.

'Venting engines. Stable landing. Rimor has landed on Haven,' said Chi. 'I'll relocate us nearer the tank when we return from the first excursion.'

In front of us was a strange world of subdued colours. The rocks were mainly dark brown, looking like sandstone, but there were grey outcrops further up the hills. The vegetation, which now looked more dark greenish-grey than black, covered the land up to about thirty metres from the water, further in some areas. Perhaps it couldn't survive isolated on the land.

'Stay, no stay?' I asked.

'Systems fine, stay,' said Chi.

Tosh looked at his scientific console, 'Stay,' he said.

'Stay,' said Mary who could see all of the ship's vital signs from Spirit's sensors.

'Okay, prepare for EVA,' I said.

We unstrapped ourselves and began to don the lightweight airtight suits. Much easier in the cramped space than the pressure suits had been on Mars.

'All sealed and checked?' I asked.

'Yes,' came from each of the others.

'Opening the inner airlock door,' I said.

We crowded into the small chamber.

'Inner door sealed,' I said.

Normally we would now open the outer airlock, but we'd put in place a contamination system. I pressed a red button on the wall. Disinfectant flooded the airlock killing any Earth bugs then the outer door swung away from the ship.

The first thing I noticed was the cold. These suits were insulated, but we were not using the heating facility as it meant we would have more time before recharging the backpacks.

I was first into the opening and feeling for the top step. The first human to set foot on a planet in another star system.

'I'm taking the pressure off all future astronauts, by not saying anything about our arrival on Haven, other than this: we all know how momentous this is, but its importance reflects the skill and knowledge of all humankind, not that of any particular individual,' I told the others.

Once we were all down the ladder, we looked down at the strange plant.

'Let's get the tethers into place,' I said.

We walked towards the tank, Bill carrying the pneumatic stapler. The tank was in good condition. The tiles had sloughed off as required and the surface was now fully exposed, ready for lift-off. The tank was as light as a feather, its weight and stability purely down to the liquid hydrogen and oxygen it contained. An examination of the engines showed that they were intact and undamaged. The legs were in good condition too and, after the disaster on Mars, extended much further than they had on the red planet. The tank had settled to just one point one degrees off vertical which was quickly compensated for by Bill using the jacks.

We picked up the ends of the tethers, took them to their maximum extension and Bill stapled them to the ground. The whole exercise took less than an hour.

Using my tablet, I signalled the device on the top of the tank and it took up the slack so that the tethers were taut.

Tosh opened his case of equipment while Chi and I examined the underside of the Rimor for any damage. The heat tiles had been stripped away by the friction of entry into the atmosphere followed by the force of the wind while we were still supersonic, exactly as planned. All the brackets and fittings had survived the journey and were ready to latch on to the tank for lift-off.

'Air looks breathable,' said Tosh, examining a small tablet attached to his atmosphere sampler.

'We won't sample it yet,' I said.

'No. I'll need to conduct microbiological tests on it first anyway. We don't want to be breathing in any pathogens,' Tosh said, peering into his microscope. 'I'll also want to test how our bacteria react with the plant. We don't want to poison any alien lifeforms. Very strange, this plant.'

'How?' I asked.

'It contains thousands of micro filaments. The dark colour makes best use of the red sunlight and the filaments appear to move water from frond to frond,' said Tosh. 'Nothing like it on Earth.'

'It's slippery too,' said Bill, grinding his shoe on a patch at the base of the tank. 'It reminds me of that horrible algae you find growing on boat slipways. Treacherous.'

'Yes, indeed,' said Tosh. 'We'll need to be careful when walking on it.'

'Any other life?' I asked.

'There are microbes, but I can't see any creepy-crawlies. I'm going to get some water samples,' Tosh said and made his way gingerly towards the shore.

Suddenly, he lost his footing and went down heavily. 'Damn it. Really slippery,' he said, getting back to his feet.

'No suit damage?' I asked.

He studied the suit environment monitor which was attached to his sleeve. 'No, no problems.'

Walking crablike, one step at a time, ensuring each foot was planted firmly before moving the other, he reached the sea. He scooped up some water into several sample flasks.

Returning to his equipment box, he put samples into his electronic microscope.

'Ha, yes. There is sea life. I can see some plankton. That suggests there are likely to be predators. The pH is 9.8 which is higher than Earth and salinity here is 1.032. That's to be expected with the longer period of land erosion Haven has probably experienced.'

'Do you want the dinghy unpacked?' asked Bill.

'I don't know,' said Tosh, half smiling, half serious. 'Not sure I want to venture onto the water in an inflatable boat until I know a little more. Don't fancy becoming dinner for a giant squid or something.'

I laughed and walked over to him. We watched these tiny shrimp-like creatures moving around in his water sample, like daphnia or copepods in pond water.

'Fascinating. Alien life on our first planet, and larger than single cells,' I said and stood up. 'Okay, Bill. Can you unpack the dinghy. Let's get out into the bay and see what coastal life there is. I presume you're not really objecting, Tosh?'

'No, of course not, it's you two who'll be in it. I'll film you getting eaten!' he said and laughed.

'We'll take care,' I said. Could there be a danger?

The dinghy was compressed into a compartment under the lander. Bill extracted it, connected it to the Rimor's pump and it gradually expanded itself, like the xenomorph in *Alien*, opening out and extending into a six-metre vessel.

Bill attached the small electric outboard motor to the rear of the boat, Tosh gave us some sample flasks, and I removed the seascope from another compartment. We waded into the shallows, trying our best not to slip on the black algae-like carpet.

We climbed in and Bill applied the power. The inflatable moved smoothly through the oily surface of the bay. About fifty metres out, Bill stopped the boat and I used the seascope to look down into the water over the side of the vessel. The seascope was an open-topped lightweight cylinder the size of an extra-large saucepan but with a glass bottom. Once it broke the surface and you looked down into it, everything beneath became clearly visible. The simplest tools were often the best.

'Anything?' asked Bill.

'The same plant seems to cover most of the rocks, but the action of the waves keeps it from covering the sand, which is more brown than yellow.

'Ah, a fishlike creature,' I said. 'Move us out another ten metres.'

The whirr of the motor pushed the boat farther from shore. Bill stopped it again and I looked back into the sea.

'More fish. Pass me the camera,' I said.

I took photographs. The animals were four to six centimetres long, torpedo shaped with a long fin running the entirety of each side. The fins rippled along the animal's whole length to create forward motion. They were quite rapid on occasion.

'Nothing any bigger?' asked Bill.

'No, just minnows. Here, have a look,' I said, passing the seascope back to him.

I surveyed the surface which stretched into the distance. It was unbroken, exhibiting only the gentlest of swells. Looking back to shore, even as the waves reached the land there was barely any breaking action.

'Crustacean,' said Bill.

I joined him at the seascope and we observed a shelled creature making its way across the sand, stopping occasionally to graze on the black algae.

'Eight legs,' said Bill. 'Like a crab, but the body is elongated similar to a lobster without claws. Seems to be feeding on the algae.'

'Whoa! Did you see that?' I asked, looking out into the bay. A distinct shape had broken the surface about two hundred metres away.

'No. What?'

'Get us back to shore. Quickly!' I shouted.

Bill returned to the tiller and the motor started, taking us deeper before turning towards shore. This time we both saw the creature break the surface.

'Wow. That's big,' said Bill, and turned the motor to full power.

Twenty seconds later the bow hit shore. We quickly climbed along it and got onto the slimy beach, pulling the inflatable behind us.

We stood and looked out to sea.

'Tosh, Chi, did you see it?' I asked.

'Yes,' said Chi arriving from down the beach. 'It looked like a seal or something.'

'No, I looked up too late,' said Tosh. 'I did warn you about giant squid!'

'I thought you were joking. Chi, did you see a head?' I asked.

'No, nothing but its back.'

'There it is again,' said Tosh, pointing down the beach to the left.

I filmed it as it swam up and down the shoreline, as if frustrated that we'd got away.

'I guessed there could be predators,' said Tosh. 'Wouldn't fancy that thing surfacing underneath the dinghy.'

'Or coming straight through it,' I agreed. I considered we'd had a near miss. 'Thank goodness we weren't any further out.'

'Think that rules out any further use of the dinghy,' said Tosh.

'Tie it up, Bill. You want to get to the ice cap, Tosh?'

'Well, one of those glaciers we spotted will do,' he replied.

'What about the air? Should we sample it?' I asked.

'Not yet, Mark,' said Tosh, examining his sampler. 'We need to remain suited until I get a clear reading on all of the trace gases and microbes.'

'Okay, keep suited up. Can you take us north, Chi?' I said.

'Sure thing, but it might be better to have a rest period now. I'd like to know we have plenty of daylight when we get onto the ice.'

We boarded Rimor and purged the air in case alien air had entered with us through the airlock. We could then strip out of our suits and sleep as best we could on our couches.

Outside, night was falling as our first day on an alien world came to an end.

19 Glacier

'Some of that plant in here,' said Tosh, as I stirred into wakefulness. He was standing by the airlock, vacuuming the black material.

'We'll have to do a spring clean before we leave the planet,' said Chi.

'Damn right,' said Tosh. 'We can't take this stuff home except under controlled conditions. There's more here.' He continued to vacuum areas near the door. 'And on our suits and boots,' he added, using a stiff brush attachment on the vacuum to clear it.

'Really?' I asked. 'Thought I'd got it off my boots.'

'This is yours?' Tosh said, holding up my left shoe. I nodded.

'We'd better use overshoes when we next go outside,' said Bill.

'Definitely,' I said, examining my boot. The plant was attached to several parts around the sole, but also above the ankle.

Tosh took it back from me and finished the cleaning process.

'Okay,' I said. 'Let's get ourselves organised, breakfasted and then set off north towards that snowfield Tosh wants to see.'

I sat on my couch and called Spirit. 'You there, Mary? Over.'

'Yes, reading you loud and clear.'

'We slept well. We've obtained dozens of plant samples and some invertebrates from the shallows,' I said.

'You using the dinghy again?' asked Mary.

'No, I don't think so. We're all a little rattled by the size of that water creature we saw. I know it's easy to overestimate sizes seen over water, but it looked the size of an elephant seal to me. Could overturn the dinghy or swamp it. We didn't see either end of it, but, presumably, it could even have been a predator wanting to make us its meal.'

'Think yourselves lucky that there's not a land version,' said Mary.

'There still could be. Look, we're preparing to jet up northwards. Tosh wants to look at thicker snow and we're hoping the planned landing spot is actually a glacier. He'd like a core as it might have trapped any creatures living on the land today or in the past.'

'Roger that. Take care,' she said. 'I got a fix on Earth, by the way.'

'Good news. We'll be careful. Will keep you in the picture. Out.'

∞∞∞∞∞∞∞∞∞∞∞

We lifted off vertically and Chi swung us out over the sea.

'Keep us low and head out over deeper water, Chi,' I said. 'I'd like to see if we can spot any of those larger animals.'

'Will do,' she said, banking us to the left and flying only twenty metres above the surface, swivelling the jets to allow us to hover over the growing swell which developed once we passed the headland.

'There!' shouted Bill.

One of the alien seal-like animals was moving along at the surface, just its back showing.

153

'And another,' Bill said pointing a little farther away.

'I'm filming. Can you get over the top of it, Chi,' said Tosh.

'Okay. Give me a minute,' Chi said, changing to vertical power and creeping towards the animal.

'Oh, good stuff,' said Tosh. I turned to look at his monitor.

The creature was just hanging at the surface now, the second one was almost directly underneath us.

Tosh and I both jumped at the same instant and recoiled as the second animal launched itself upwards. '*Up!*' I shouted. There was a clang against the hull and the creature fell back into the water as Chi gained altitude.

'What the devil was that?' she asked.

'It attacked us,' I said.

'What with?'

'Its teeth!' I said.

'Look, there's six of them down there now, circling like a pack of sharks,' said Tosh.

'What was our altitude when that thing hit us?' I asked.

Chi checked her readings. 'Eighteen metres.'

'Eighteen metres!' I said in astonishment. 'It jumped eighteen metres vertically out of the water?'

'It did,' said Tosh. 'I've got it in slo-mo.'

We watched a second individual launch itself skywards, but it didn't reach us this time and fell back in a cascade of spray.

'What's the altitude now, Chi?' I asked.

'Thirty metres.'

While Chi continued to fly us north, Bill, Tosh and I huddled around his video screen watching the first sequence.

The two animals were circling each other, then, with no warning at all, the second animal leapt into the air. The whole thing was blue-grey in colour. Its front end was rounded, like a Beluga whale. There was no sign of any eyes, but a slit across the front opened and four tusks materialised, one from each corner of the mouth. We saw it shudder as it struck the hull and fell back, creating an enormous splash as it hit the water and vanished into the depths.

'I don't believe that,' said Bill. 'Thank God we got back to shore quickly yesterday.'

'For sure,' I said with a shudder. 'I think we'll use the ROV[5] in the sea when we return. These things seem to be top of the food chain. We need to study them.'

'Did you notice its fins?' asked Tosh, 'Although they were flattened against its sides as it jumped, they were the same as the ones you filmed on the smaller fish. Seems to be a single fin running along each side.'

'Hey! What are you guys looking at?' asked Chi, unable to see the screen.

'It's a vicious looking thing with tusks,' said Bill. 'It's what hit our underside, Chi.'

'What, at eighteen metres?' she asked. 'The whole animal? I thought you meant it had hurled a projectile.'

'No. The whole animal leapt up at us. Staggering,' Bill replied.

---

[5] Remote Operated Vehicle for studying underwater environments.

'How the hell did it produce that thrust? It must have weighed at least a ton. Did you see a tail?' I asked.

'Yes, at least a ton. No tail, no,' said Tosh.

'I'd like to see the spot it hit when we land,' said Bill. 'Those tusks were sharp. It could have damaged the hull.'

'Hull integrity is one hundred per cent,' said Chi.

'The camera's still working, so it didn't hit that,' said Tosh.

'I'm staggered by the power we've just witnessed,' I said. 'Do you think we're safe at the landing site?'

'I'm sure it could sling itself out of the water to where we landed last time,' said Tosh.

'Chi, when we return, give us another thirty metres from the shoreline,' I said.

'Okay,' she said, 'but we can't do anything to relocate the tank.'

'Well, we're not living in the tank,' said Bill.

'How long to the glacier?' I asked.

'Twenty minutes,' said Chi.

'I'd like to watch that again, Tosh,' I said. The three of us peered at the monitor, trying to figure out what had given the creature such incredible propulsion. This wasn't a low mass world. Gravity was similar to that on Earth.

∞∞∞∞∞∞∞∞∞∞

'That's the location,' said Tosh as Rimor crossed the snow-covered ridge and a glacier came into view. It was narrow here, only a couple of hundred metres, with bare rock either side. Of course, with the colour of the sun, the ice and snow had a pink tinge to it. The sky remained a dark bluish purple.

156

'There's a patch of clear land on our right,' said Chi. 'Can you climb down from there?'

'Why not land on the glacier?' Tosh asked.

'Landing gear could get stuck in the ice,' Chi replied.

'Okay,' said Tosh. 'Can you set us down as near the ice as possible?'

'Sure thing,' she said. We banked to the right and settled gently on the hillside. 'Okay, jacking up left struts to level us.'

The lander, which had been at a rather rakish angle, gradually levelled itself.

'Okay. Down,' said Chi. 'Spirit. We've landed.'

'Copy you down,' said Mary.

'Thought you'd cleaned my boot,' I said, examining some plant on the side of the sole.

'I did,' said Tosh.

'Well, it's back again, then,' I said.

Bill examined his boots. 'Yes, grown again on mine too.'

'We'll need to do a deep clean before we leave Haven,' said Tosh.

In the cramped cockpit of the Rimor, it was a bit of a crowd to get into our suits. We charged our backpacks from the ship's air and power supplies, pulled on disposable overshoes and made our way, one at a time, down onto the bare rocky hillside.

'I'll take some rock samples while you're on the glacier,' I said.

'Bring two or three core rods please, Bill,' said Tosh as he headed down the slope onto the ice.

As a geologist, I was in my element here. I saw what I recognised as tourmaline in the lighter veins of the rocky outcrop. No sign of the black plant here. It seemed fairly sterile.

I chiselled out some samples. The main metamorphic hillside held a lot of cassiterite, probably in minable concentrations. Nothing too dissimilar from Earth. I soon had twenty different samples and closed my case.

I looked back to the ship. Chi was underneath, examining the damage inflicted by our tusked sea creature. She saw me looking at her, 'Nothing serious,' she said over the suit communicator. 'Dented the hull, though.'

I gave her a thumbs-up, placed my rocks in the airlock and joined her under the hull. There were three clear dents in the hull. Pointed depressions.

'If we'd been lower, I think it could have penetrated,' I said.

'Yes, not good. Let's hope there are no land versions,' said Chi.

'We haven't seen any land animals at all. If that means there is no prey, then it would likely mean no predators, I should think,' I said.

'I'm still checking three-sixty for mountain lions and pterodactyls. Need to take care,' she said.

I turned towards the glacier. Tosh and Bill were obtaining ice cores and I made my way over to them.

'How deep's the ice?'

'Sonar says twelve metres here,' replied Tosh. 'We're just taking sections of cores, rather than the whole thing, to keep the weight down.'

A piece of hemp cloth lay on the surface beside them with a growing number of ten centimetre core samples.

'Anything unusual?' I asked.

'What? Apart from the fact that this is ice on an Earth-like planet forty light years from home!' he said, exhibiting his well-known disagreeable nature when his work was questioned. I'd known him long enough not to take offence. I knew he would want to share his findings, but on his terms.

A minute later, he said, 'There's nothing in the way of airborne creatures, but this is interesting.' Using tongs, he picked up a still intact core of ice, one centimetre in diameter and some forty centimetres long, and showed it to me. 'Do you see the regular layers of dark grey specks?'

'Yes,' I said. 'What are they?'

'I'll have to do some analysis, but it looks like pollen to me. Until we know how long it takes to lay down this glacial ice, we won't know how long it is between these layers being deposited until I've done some more work on it. I'd guess that it is a seasonal deposit.'

'Interesting,' I said. 'Haven has no appreciable axis tilt, so there shouldn't be seasons. Wonder what triggers the pollen production.'

'How eccentric is the orbit?' he asked.

'Almost circular. No seasonal effect there either.'

'Life cycle of the plant, I assume,' said Tosh. 'I'm guessing that it comes from the seaweed, unless there are major areas of plants we've not seen from orbit.'

'Do the layers run the length of the cores?' I asked.

159

'Yes. Bill counted sixty in this one core. It is extremely regular. Other than that, nothing of any immediate interest, but the microscope is sure to reveal much more.'

'How long, before you're finished?'

'As long as it takes,' he snapped.

'Roughly?'

'We're almost there. Twenty minutes,' he said, looking around at Bill who was operating the corer. 'Bill, how long before you have that one?'

'Any minute, then one more to do on the far side,' Bill said, waving his arm towards the other side of the glacier, perhaps two hundred metres away.

'Chi's nervous about mountain lions and pterodactyls,' I said. 'Keep checking your surroundings. You never know. That thing in the water unnerved me too.'

I returned to the Rimor, examined the dents in the polymer strengthened hull again, then stood and took in the view.

The mountains were mainly rounded, suggesting that mountain building had not been happening for millions of years. Over to the west were a few more dramatic peaks, but nothing like as young and jagged as the mountains found on Earth.

Turning the other way, the glacier was a tributary to a much larger ice sheet in the valley below. It, in turn, continued into the far distance where it stopped, relatively suddenly, a kilometre or two before the sea, as usual black fringed by the strange seaweed which had adapted itself to make use of the red sunlight and its strong infrared component.

Beautiful and magnificent, but in a desolate sort of way. I couldn't wait to get back to base. Tomorrow I intended to get the ROV out into deeper water, for there we knew there was life – sophisticated, and undoubtedly dangerous animal life.

20 Undersea

'Damn it,' said Chi. 'There's some of that plant on my control panel.'

'Yes,' said Bill, 'and on my couch.'

'Some here too,' said Tosh.

'Okay. We'll have to have a deep clean before we leave, but use disinfected wipes on any you see in here before we suit up,' I said.

'My atmospheric test has come back all-clear. We don't need to wear suits. There were no adverse effects on the plant or the plankton from our exhaled atmosphere or shipboard bacteria either. What do you want to do?' Tosh asked.

'Okay, no suits. Our flight suits will do,' I said.

'That'll make it easier to work,' said Tosh.

'Yes. Wear throat mikes though,' I said.

'All ready? I'm lifting off in four, three, two, one,' said Chi and we felt the jets pushing us off the rocky outcrop, the undercarriage withdrew, and we flew into the mountains.

'Still no land plants,' said Bill.

'No, but look at that lake down there. Black as coal and fringed with the same weed we encountered on the coast,' said Chi.

'Mark. Can we stop there?' said Tosh. 'I need specimens. We should find out if it is the same species or a freshwater variation.'

'Take us down, Chi,' I said, 'but at least fifty metres from the water.'

'Will do,' she said and banked to the right, circled the lake, found a suitable flat area, and we were down. 'Spirit. Come in please.'

'Mary here, Chi,' came the reply.

'Note this location. Freshwater lake. Tosh wants samples. We're also going out without suits.'

'Copy that,' said Mary.

The next hour was spent using disinfected wipes to clear the plant. There was more of it than we'd realised. Amazing that it was apparently rooting itself to metal and plastic. What was somewhat worrying was that it could be developing inside equipment consoles.

We climbed out of the airlock and sampled the air.

'Ugh!' I said. 'What is that smell? It's familiar.'

'Smells like an old blanket which has been left to fester in a shed or garage,' Bill said. 'When you move it, that is exactly the sort of stink it produces.'

'Yes. Unpleasant,' I said.

'Stop moaning,' said Tosh. 'In five minutes you'll hardly notice it.'

'It's okay,' said Chi. 'Interesting, and at least it's real, not canned, like our sanitised ship's air. Alien air. How privileged are we to be smelling real alien air? Growing up in Hong Kong, as a kid I remember hundreds of different aromas, from the cooking, the streets, the sea. Big part of my childhood.'

'Well, you can keep this one,' I said. 'Bill's nailed it – a damp festering blanket which has been lying in a shed for years.' I laughed.

While Tosh and Bill set about examining the water and checking if this was a different species of plant, Chi came with me up onto the hill where I could sample the regolith and rocks. Tosh was right, of course. We soon forgot the musty smell of the air.

The rocks here were metamorphic, speckled with mineral crystals. I took eight samples, bagged them and turned, with Chi, to look back at the others.

'It's the green I miss,' said Chi, sadly.

'Yes. I guess we could plant grass and shrubs here,' I said.

'But would they survive in this red sunlight?' she asked.

'More importantly, that weed might overwhelm other plants. If it grew over their leaves they'd soon die,' I mused. 'I wonder if we could eat it.'

'I expect that it would need processing,' said Chi.

In the distance, Tosh and Bill were out in the dinghy. Having taken water samples, they were heading back to shore and ran the boat up the beach.

When Chi and I joined them, Bill had attached the dinghy to the ship and was vacuuming the air out of it, preparing to store it back in its locker.

'No creature from the black lagoon, then?' I asked.

'No large animal could live in a lake that small,' said Tosh.

'I was being facetious!'

'Never!' he retorted.

'Come see this, Mark,' Bill called over to me.

I leaned over the dinghy and we looked into its locker.

'It's covered,' I said.

'Must have been a lot on the boat when I stored it back at the base camp,' said Bill.

'Tosh,' I called. 'Your advice is required.'

Tosh meandered over to the locker. 'My God! That's not good. The entire compartment is covered in the stuff.'

'How do we get rid of it?' asked Bill. 'Probably did better in here owing to the damp fabric of the boat.'

'Well,' Tosh said, 'it's too big a job for wipes.'

'Antibacterial spray?' I asked.

'Yes, that would do the job, but we don't have a huge supply,' said Tosh, running his finger across it and clearing a stripe. 'It does come off easy enough. I'd leave it for now. No point in spending an age clearing the stuff now when it is likely to gain a foothold again back at base. My entity is happy with what we're doing.'

'Okay, same with mine,' I agreed. 'Stow the dinghy as it is, Bill.'

∞∞∞∞∞∞∞∞∞∞

'Come in, Spirit,' said Chi.

'Copy you, Chi,' said Anna.

'Just lifting off from the lake. We're planning to fly over the watershed of this range of hills, then follow the river system back to the sea. I'll let you know if we land anywhere en route.'

'Copy that, Chi. Out,' said Anna.

What a pleasure to breathe our own air again. Chi really didn't seem to mind it, but I hated the mustiness. It smelled positively unhealthy to me.

The jets fired and we lifted vertically. We continued up to the mountain ridge, selected a drainage valley and followed it down the hillside. As soon as the meltwater emerged from the foot of the glacier, it was fringed with the black plant all of the way to the sea.

Chi banked us left and we followed the coastline, watching for water creatures at the surface, but saw none. Eventually, the orange colour of our fuel tank came into view and Chi parked us well away from the shore.

'How's fuel?' I asked.

'Okay for a couple more trips, but aren't you going to need me to fly you out over the sea to deploy the ROV?' Chi asked.

'Yes,' said Bill. 'We certainly can't deploy it from the dinghy. Don't fancy tackling those beasts on their home turf.'

'Good point,' I agreed.

'In that case,' said Chi, 'the deployment will be the last trip. I have no intention of trying to dock with the tank when short of fuel.'

'Okay. You're the boss when it comes to the Rimor,' I said. 'I'm wearing a suit this time, didn't like the smell of that air.'

'Yes, me too,' said Bill.

When we climbed down onto the land, only Chi decided to go without her suit. She said that she thought breathing the air was "all part of the experience".

∞∞∞∞∞∞∞∞∞∞

Bill unpacked the ROV. It was bright yellow and about the size of a small refrigerator. Propellers were set into each of the corners and cameras were on the forward end

166

as well as the sides and bottom. Powerful spotlights were set on either side of the front camera. I'd used these things before on Earth to study underwater geological structures. It was wonderful technology.

'Not well camouflaged,' joked Chi.

'No, but yellow is particularly good in water. You can see the submersible's yellow body long before you'd see any other colour,' Tosh explained.

'Learn something new every day,' she said. 'The Beatles *Yellow Submarine* was less funny than we all thought, then.'

'Well, Ringo probably didn't know the science,' said Bill and laughed.

'Didn't they use a yellow submarine at Loch Ness, to look for the monster?' I asked.

'Yes, I think they did,' said Bill, 'and we're going to use this one to film monsters too.'

'Hope we have better luck than them,' said Tosh.

We lifted the machine and attached it to a release bracket under the Rimor. The monitoring console we positioned under the tank framework. Once we were set up, Chi flew the Rimor out to sea, hovered just above the surface, released the submersible, and immediately gained height. She'd told me she wasn't going to give the larger beasts time to plan an attack.

All of a sudden, the monitor was showing an underwater scene.

'Wonder if they'll get curious,' mused Bill.

'Depends how hungry they are,' I said. 'What's the depth here, Tosh?'

'We have ten metres beneath us, so about fifteen metres in total. Plenty of those fish.'

A shoal of fish passed before the submersible. They had a passing resemblance to wrasse, but with fins either side instead of top and bottom. Very beautiful, the way they moved, but no colour to them.

One of the side cameras showed a collection nozzle coming out of the ROV. Tosh activated the suction and made a fast run at the shoal. 'Got 'em!' he cried. 'Two of them.'

The collection tube stored itself again and the submersible cruised the bottom, moving deeper and following the descending terrain. Surface light was now gone and the machine was relying on its own illumination.

'Twenty metres deep here. Something bigger ahead,' Tosh said, and we saw sediment disturbed as an eel-like creature vanished into the murk.

Suddenly, the picture turned somersault. '*What the hell was that?*' exclaimed Bill.

'Something hit us,' said Tosh.

The ROV righted itself and then a large grey shape passed in front of the camera.

'How big?' I asked.

'At least six metres. Bulky too. Possibly one of the beasts,' said Tosh as the ROV was buffeted again.

'They don't like it,' said Chi, who had landed the Rimor and come to see how things were going.

'Whoa!' shouted Tosh, as the vehicle was attacked again.

This time we got a good view of the tusks on one side of the animal as it charged the left side of the machine.

'Can it hurt it?' asked Chi.

'Unlikely,' Tosh said. 'I'm arming biopsy cannon one.'

A small tube, about two centimetres in diameter could be seen extending to the right of the main camera.

'Come on, you beauty, just cross in front of us again,' whispered Tosh, as if the animals could hear him.

'Will it hurt it?' asked Chi.

'If they feel pain, it will certainly nip,' said Tosh. 'Won't do any permanent damage though.'

The buffeting and charging continued. The animals certainly believed this thing was invading their territory. Then one of them passed the front of the ROV and I saw Tosh hit a red button on the console.

In a flash, the biopsy dart hit the animal and withdrew back into the hull with its core sample of skin and flesh. The animal twisted and violently headed upwards. In the distance we saw it clear the surface by a good ten metres and crash back down into the water.

'That upset it!' I said.

'Too right,' agreed Bill.

We didn't see any more of the large beasts as we continued to examine the silty bottom and record images of other marine life.

'That's odd,' said Tosh. 'None of the others have approached, if they're there.'

'Maybe the one you harpooned warned them off?' Chi asked.

'That would be rather profound,' he said.

'Wonder if they have a language?' I asked.

'I presume not,' said Tosh, 'but the hydrophone is picking up some noises. We'll need to analyse it back home.'

On one occasion, a one-metre-long creature with tentacles, like a squid, passed by. Tosh got a tissue sample from it and was also able to collect several molluscs and a crablike creature.

'Batteries below fifteen per cent,' said Bill.

'I think we'll call it a day,' Tosh said and pressed an auto-homing button. The ROV would now find its way to the closest point on the shoreline.

Twenty minutes later it drove itself ashore.

'Leave it sitting there for a while,' I said.

Tosh looked at me, puzzled.

'Those beasts might be intelligent enough to associate it with the Rimor. Don't want to get skewered while we're carrying it up that slippery shoreline.'

'Yes. Hadn't thought of that,' said Tosh.

Later, while we were half carrying, half dragging the submersible up the shoreline, a couple of the beasts did appear in the bay, their front ends visible as if they were watching us, although we could see no obvious eyes. I felt a lot better when we'd reached the Rimor and Tosh could begin transferring his specimens to storage cases.

'Okay. Trappist-1 is setting. Last night sleeping in the Rimor,' I said, 'then tomorrow we'll clean up and leave.'

'Won't miss this place,' said Bill.

'Heathen!' said Tosh loudly. 'We found a habitable planet with indigenous life on our very first attempt. It's amazing.'

'Suppose so,' said Bill, 'but I really don't like the place. Sorry. You won't catch me on the first wagon train to colonise it.'

21 Preparing to Leave

Next morning, we had to pack and clean up. Getting rid of the alien plant would not be easy. We all wore suits, although Chi continued to prefer to breathe the air and had her visor open. I really didn't like the smell. I still couldn't quite pin down the aroma. The closest I could get was rotting vegetation or that similarity to a mouldy old blanket which Bill had suggested.

Bill and Chi removed a substantial shelter from one of the Rimor lockers and had it erected in about an hour. It was similar to, but larger and stronger than the one we had erected on Mars.

They fixed it to the bedrock some sixty metres from the shore, to be out of range of the sea creatures and any future floods. Inside we stored all of the equipment which would not be accompanying us back into orbit. Weight was critical, of course. The dinghy, ROV, the unused buggy, and almost all of our sampling equipment and microscopes were put in the cache, which should be secure for many years, to be used by any returning expeditions. Several long-term experiments were also set up. The data could be collected from orbit by any returning expeditions.

'That's it all stored, Mark,' said Bill, returning to the Rimor.

'I wonder if we ever will colonise this place,' Chi said.

'Don't know. That plant is so invasive. We would have to find a way to control or eradicate it,' I said. 'Otherwise I'm sure it would smother any Earth crops.'

'Yes. Possibly,' agreed Tosh, finishing his scrubbing of the dinghy's storage locker. 'I think this is clean.'

Bill and I examined the interior, giving one or two areas a vigorous rub with wet wipes. We then sealed the compartment. The lockers had vents which could be left open and we did that in order to allow the vacuum of space to finish the weed destruction process. The ice cores, rock, plant, fish and invertebrate samples had their own double-sealed containers.

'Hey, look!' shouted Tosh.

We all turned to look along the shoreline. A strange, grey mist was rising from the beach. We watched in amazement as it rose vertically from the seaweed along the entire coastline before being carried away on a light offshore breeze.

'What do you make of that?' I asked.

'Could be pollen or something. Maybe that's how it reproduces,' said Tosh, who ran towards the shore with a couple of sampling containers. 'I need to get specimens.'

'Don't slip,' Bill shouted, but by then Tosh was already swinging his sample bags in arcs around his head and body.

'I can smell it,' said Chi, who still had her visor open. 'It has a certain sweetness to it.'

The breeze was now onshore and the grey mist was moving towards us. 'Shut your faceplate, quickly!' I said.

'I have, but it isn't unpleasant. Uncharacteristic, really,' she said. 'Would have expected such a nasty plant to produce something less aromatic.'

I watched her breathing and blinking to be sure there was no effect on her eyes. Suddenly the expression on her face changed from one of detached interest to one of absolute horror.

'Quick. Check my seals! *Now!*' she shouted, double checking her visor. I ran over to her and helped her tighten the shoulder rings.

'What's up?' asked Tosh, running towards us to help.

'I can't feel anything wrong but my entity is really alarmed and says the air is deadly,' said Chi.

'But it's almost Earth-like,' said Tosh. 'No harmful chemicals or gases. No pathogens or dangerous bacteria.'

'Tosh, you're covered in the stuff,' I said, looking at the grey powder which coated his suit. He wiped his visor with his glove to clear it.

'You are too,' said Tosh.

'My entity tells me these are spores and she's having trouble fighting them off. They're in my mouth, nose, throat and lungs,' said Chi, beginning to become panicky and starting to cough.

'Flush your suit out,' said Tosh. 'Open the valve and hyperventilate while the canned air pushes out the alien atmosphere.'

I watched Chi obeying Tosh's instructions.

Chi coughed again and again while the backpack blew fresh air through her suit.

'How's it feel now?' asked Tosh.

'I still can't feel anything wrong, except an irritation in my mouth and lungs. Doesn't seem to be bad,' she said, 'but my ent is still panicking. Never known her behave like this.'

'Look at the way it is settling on us,' said Bill.

'Can we do anything to help, Chi?' Tosh asked, putting his arm around her shoulders.

Chi didn't answer immediately, perhaps she was "speaking" to her entity. 'No. She says there's nothing, but she's warning about the pollen. I'll let her speak.'

Chi's eyes glazed over as the entity took over control of her body and speech centres. 'It is attacking the inside of our body. Lungs and mouth, also getting into our digestive tract.'

'How are you fighting it?' Tosh asked.

'It is burning. Getting in by burning the tissue. I can stop it, but not completely. I've got a mass of white blood cells rushing to each incursion, but they're having trouble keeping up.'

'Antibiotics? I have a small supply of a very powerful antibiotic on board,' said Tosh.

'No. Wouldn't help.' Chi coughed and we saw a trickle of blood from the corner of her mouth. 'It is penetrating my permeable membranes. Especially in the alveoli and bronchia.'

'You're bleeding,' I said.

'I'm losing it,' she said, coughing again. More blood was being ejected and sticking to the inside of the visor. 'We're dying. Can't stop it!'

'Tosh?' I looked at him for ideas. I could see the anguish in his face. He had no solution.

He pulled Chi tighter to him. 'There's nothing I can do. Try a second air flush.'

'Help me!' said Chi. Tosh punched the correct buttons on Chi's forearm and we heard the backpack purging the suit air again. She coughed twice more and her visor was completely splattered with blood. 'No. No, we're losing the fight?' came, I assumed, from the entity, punctuated by coughing fits.

'Chi. No. No. Can I do anything at all?' said Tosh, holding both of her arms and trying to peer into her helmet.

Chi crumpled to the ground, pulling Tosh over with her and we could hear continual coughing, gurgling and choking. 'Drowning!' she spluttered. Her body thrashed about on the ground for almost two minutes, then the movement became less violent, her chest stopped heaving and she stilled.

'Chi. Chi!' Tosh said, frantically shaking her. 'Darling. Speak to me.'

No response. Tosh let go. 'Chi!' I shouted, cradling her head and trying to see past the blood splattered visor. There was no movement. No breathing. I purged her suit again.

'I think we've lost her,' said Bill, pulling on my arm. 'Let her go, Mark.'

I sat back on the ground. Tosh cradled Chi in his arms. Bill stood, looking down at her, helpless. No one spoke for at least a minute. We were all in shock over her death. So fast, and nothing we could do to stop it.

'We can't let this pollen into the Rimor,' said Bill, eventually.

'And how are we going to manage to get in ourselves?' I said. 'We're covered in the damn stuff.' I brushed it off my suit. A few grains of this stuff in the spacecraft could kill us all. 'It's no wonder there are no land animals on this world.'

'Can't imagine a worse way to die,' said Bill, choking back tears as he spoke. He looked back towards the shoreline. 'Whatever it was, it seems to have stopped.' Bill pointed towards the sea.

I looked around. The grey mist was completely gone and no more was being ejected from the weed. It must have been a rare occurrence. We'd been unlucky. Any other day and we might never have even known about it.

'I'll wager that is what we'll find when we analyse those layers in Tosh's ice core samples,' said Bill, recovering his composure. 'It must occur on some sort of regular basis when certain conditions are right.'

We all stared in silence at the sea for a long time. We'd lost Chi. However, the dreadful truth was that we were all in the same danger. We dared not take any of this pollen, or the plant, into the Rimor and we hadn't even begun to clean the cabin. I turned back to Chi. Tosh was sitting on the ground, sobbing, with her lying against his chest, the visor completely covered with her blood.

'The Rimor's covered in the stuff too,' said Bill.

'Yes, and the bottom half of the tank,' I said.

'I'll go and get the spade from the shelter,' said Bill.

'Yes,' I mused. 'We need to bury her. Help me strip her out of the suit. Bring a couple of spades, Bill.'

'Any point in stripping her. The suit is made to measure, anyway,' said Bill.

'Suppose so,' I said. 'It just seems wrong, somehow, to leave her in the suit.'

Bill returned and began to dig an area which had no plant on it, just beyond the boundary of its domain.

'It'll preserve her better than a coffin,' Tosh said. 'I think she might prefer that. Being an astronaut was her life.'

We each took turns until we had a hole about one and a half metres deep by two long, by about sixty centimetres wide.

'What about her entity?' said Bill.

'How do you mean?' asked Tosh.

'Did it die with her?'

'Hadn't thought of that,' I said.

'We'd better open her up, Mark,' said Tosh.

I really didn't fancy that, but we all felt it was important to check. Our entities were part of each of us, our friends and personal assistants.

'Just open the visor,' Bill said.

I undid the seals and slid the visor up carefully. Chi's dead face came into view, completely covered in congealing blood. Her eyes were open and so was her mouth but filled with blood. Her face was locked in the grimace of someone who has drowned. No sign of the entity. Tosh closed her eyes.

My own entity suggested I tap on Chi's forehead.

Nothing. No movement, no sign of her entity emerging. Mine suggested that it must have died with her. I told the others. There was a consensus that we leave the visor open for an hour while we worked out how to clean the outside of the Rimor. We could then make a final check for the entity.

We certainly didn't want any of the plant or pollen making its way back to Spirit.

178

'I'd better let the others know,' I said.

Bill and Tosh nodded.

'I'll take a sample of her blood,' said Tosh.

I switched to my main radio. 'Hello, Rimor here, come in, Spirit, over.'

Almost a minute passed before the answer came. 'Spirit here, copy you. We've been busy studying planet F. It was at closest approach just now, over,' said Anna.

'Sorry, we have some very bad news. Are you both there, over,' I said.

'Copy that, Mark. Both here. What's up?' Mary said.

'We've lost Chi.'

'How do you mean "lost"?' asked Anna.

'She's dead. The weed produces a deadly pollen.'

'What? And it killed her?' asked Mary.

'In a matter of minutes. Not nice. Her entity did its best. She drowned in her own blood.'

'God, no!' said Anna. 'How awful.'

'It seemed to attack her lungs, mouth, throat and gullet. Her entity tried everything to stop it. It killed her entity as well.'

'Oh God! How's Tosh?' said Mary.

'As you might expect.'

'Tosh, we're so sorry. You'll need to ensure you don't bring any back with you,' said Mary.

'Samples are in sealed containers,' Tosh said, 'but the pollen is absolutely everywhere.'

'Right,' said Anna. 'Let us know how it goes. Can't believe she's dead.'

'No. We're pretty upset down here too,' said Bill.

'Yes, us too,' said Mary. 'Let us know how the cleaning goes. We'll give it some thought up here as well.'

We had to get to work.

From the wing above us, Bill said, 'I've brushed it all off the fuselage, wings and engines. A light spray should be enough, but it would be better to leave it until just before we depart.'

'Vacuum should kill it as soon as we reach orbit,' I said.

'When I tested the plant,' said Tosh, 'it didn't survive vacuum, but I don't know about the pollen and I don't want to open the airlock to get the vacuum test equipment until we know we're leaving. Don't forget that there's some tech we need to stow in the shelter before we leave, and it's inside.'

'I'd be tempted to throw it out of the airlock to save further contamination,' I said.

'If we're going to do that, then we can use the dump airlock,' said Bill.

'Right,' I said. The one-way dump airlock was accessible from the floor of the cabin. It allowed us to jettison anything into space or, if done here, onto the surface.

We pulled out the two disinfectant spray pumps which we could connect to the containers. After a minute pumping up the pressure, it provided about ten minutes of spraying action.

Working with the spray and some disposable cloths, I cleaned six lockers. Bill was attacking the lockers on the other side and Tosh was removing traces from the undercarriage and the landing gear storage compartments.

'Only two containers of disinfectant remaining,' said Bill. 'Do you think it's enough?'

'You managing to sterilise the inside of the Rimor?' asked Mary from Spirit.

'We've been dealing with the outside first,' I replied. 'We still haven't worked out how we're going to get through the airlock without contaminating the ship. We've only got two containers of disinfectant remaining.'

'Manoeuvring fuel is a pretty effective steriliser. Use it to give a final spray to the outside areas,' said Mary.

'It won't do any harm inside, either,' said Anna. 'Spray it everywhere inside the Rimor then purge it with fresh air. Wait ten minutes and purge it again. Should kill anything inside. Leave the internal airlock door open. It will ensure the airlock is sterile too.'

'We won't be exiting through this airlock again. What about the printed circuitry and other electronics?' I asked.

'It evaporates very quickly,' said Anna. 'As long as you leave everything switched off until after the second purge, you should be okay.'

'The Rimor is oversupplied with manoeuvring fuel. You can draw at least ten kilos to spray the craft, as long as you make a sensible orbit altitude,' said Anna.

'What are you doing about Chi?' asked Mary.

'We've buried her in her suit,' Bill said.

'Say a few words for us,' she said.

'Chi wasn't religious,' said Tosh. 'She wouldn't want any ceremony.'

'Okay, but say something anyway, for us,' said Mary. 'Take care. Let us know how you are going to get in without bringing any of the pollen.'

'You okay with docking, Mark?' asked Anna.

'Chi said there was plenty of fuel left,' I said.

'You did okay in the simulator,' said Anna, guessing that I was feeling apprehensive.

'How's the weather looking down here? Wind speed? Any weather approaching?' I asked.

'Light. Under five kph,' said Anna. 'That's almost dead still. Nothing bad forecast.'

'Right,' I said.

'You'll be fine,' said Anna.

'I'll let you know how we're doing,' I said.

'Don't forget the tank guy ropes,' said Anna.

'I won't. I'll call you before we enter the ship to check I've not missed anything on the outside checklist, because I don't have it with me.'

'I'll send a copy to your tablet.'

'No good. It's inside the Rimor and there's no way we're leaving again once we're inside,' I said.

'No, I suppose not. Okay, ask again when you're ready and I'll run through it with you,' said Anna.

The three of us walked over to Chi's grave, made a final check that her entity wasn't on her head anywhere. Tosh wiped her visor clean, then sealed her faceplate and we filled the hole.

Tosh hammered a metal slab into the ground at the head of the grave. He'd painted, 'HERE LIES CHI

WANG. MUCH LOVED ENHANCED HUMAN PILOT FROM THE PLANET EARTH,' in red paint.

'Sorry,' he said, 'red was the only colour in the maintenance locker.'

'I don't know what to say,' I said.

'I do,' said Bill.

'Hello, Spirit. Are you listening?' I said.

'Yes. We're here,' said Mary.

Bill moved around to behind the metal slab, stood to attention and said, 'We are gathered here to commit astronaut Chi Wang and her entity to the ground. Chi was an essential component of the first spolding missions to Mars and Trappist-1; she will be sorely missed.'

I heard a couple of anonymous murmurs of 'Amen,' over the radio.

'Right, Anna. What's the outside checklist?' I asked.

'Detach tank guy ropes; remove tank leg securing pins; check docking fixings are clear of any tile remnants or other debris; close all lockers; visual check of the tank; visual check of the Rimor; extra check of the docking brackets and fuel supply pipe covers,' said Anna.

'Come with me, Bill,' I said.

We both double-checked all of the crucial external items then had to think about how best to get into the Rimor?

'Open the airlock, Bill,' I said.

The door was swung open and we could see that the plant had, once again, gained a foothold. Tosh climbed the ladder and carried out a thorough spray with the disinfectant. Meanwhile, I drained some manoeuvring jet fuel into one of the empty disinfectant containers, passed it to Tosh and he gave the airlock another thorough spray.

'Right, now spray us, Tosh,' I said.

The spray was turned on Bill and me and we were meticulously rinsed down. Two more containers were filled. Bill showered Tosh and we all climbed up to the airlock. We kicked off our overshoes and sprayed our boots a second time. Bill sprayed all components of the door and we pulled it shut behind us.

Tosh opened the inner door of the airlock. We were shocked at the amount of plant we found growing on surfaces inside. We used an entire container of fuel spraying everywhere. On Anna's advice we stood and moved around in the Rimor for an hour. This would allow the fumes to penetrate the equipment consoles and our suit joints. We removed our three full-pressure suits from the internal storage area, sprayed the exteriors of the suits, opened them and sprayed the insides too.

'Computer, purge the atmosphere from the Rimor,' I said.

'Atmosphere purging, Mark.'

Five minutes later, the computer said, 'Purging complete, Mark.'

'Computer, do any chemicals remain in the atmosphere?'

'Traces of jet fuel and disinfectant, Mark.'

'Computer, purge again,' I said.

'That will reduce reserves of air to thirty-eight per cent, Mark.'

'Okay. Do it anyway,' I said.

We heard the pumps straining again.

'Purge complete, Mark.'

I gingerly opened my faceplate. No smell at all. One at a time, we removed our suits, were disinfected by each other and put them into the dump airlock, together with all the other equipment which we should have been leaving in the storage tent on the planet. Who would ever check? After our experience, I was beginning to think we might be the first and last people to ever visit Haven. How dreadfully we'd misnamed it.

We now climbed into our full-pressure suits and took our seats. I was certainly not looking forward to what came next.

Just when I was ready and had resolved to get the docking job done, I noticed something I hadn't expected, sitting fairly and squarely on top of the pilot's console. It immediately brought me to tears. Shooey. How dreadful. We hadn't been able to leave her toy in the grave beside her, to assist her in her journey through eternity. It's luck had not extended to fighting off an alien pathogen.

'Can you stow that thing, Bill?' I said, pointing at it.

'Surely,' he said, unstrapping himself from the commander's seat beside me.

'No,' said Tosh. 'Give it to me. I'll look after it.' The strange Chinese toy was passed back to Tosh. I didn't see what he did with it. It took a few minutes for me to compose myself again.

Although I had flown the Rimor and docked it with the tank at least a dozen times in the simulator, I had never done it for real, nor in a pressure suit, and my nerves jangled with apprehension. Lift-off wouldn't be a problem, but first I had to fly it into a vertical position and dock with the tank. The automatic system could do it, but if anything went wrong, I'd have to step in and finish the job manually.

'Computer, how much fuel remains?' I asked.

'Twelve per cent, Mark.'

Enough for a couple of attempts, but not quite enough for three.

'Anna, what's the launch window like?' I asked.

'Your launch window has just opened. Anytime in the next two hours. We'll manoeuvre to a rendezvous location when we've seen you heading towards orbit.'

'Copy that, Anna,' I said. 'All strapped in? Prepare for docking.'

Such relief when I heard the engines fire. I pulled back on the stick and we rose vertically to about ten metres. The undercarriage rose, I flew us around to the docking side of the tank and brought up the nose to vertical.

'Okay, computer. Dock us,' I said.

'Beginning docking procedure,' said the computer.

Some of the tension left my body when I heard the docking clamps attaching and four green lights lit on my dashboard.

'Docking complete,' said the computer. 'Hoses connecting.'

We could hear the pumps injecting the fuel under pressure from the main tank.

Five minutes later. 'Both fuel tanks one hundred per cent,' the computer confirmed.

'Ready for lift-off?' I asked.

Bill and Tosh replied in the affirmative. For a moment I was waiting for Chi to speak, but I wouldn't ever hear her gentle Chinese accent again.

'Five, four, three, two, ignition,' I said, and we felt the huge power of the tank and Rimor's combined engines under full thrust.

22 Orbit

Reaching orbit gave incredible relief. It showed the importance of our continual mission training, even for situations we were never likely to experience.

'Well done, Mark,' said Bill.

'Hello, Rimor. We have you in view,' said Anna. 'We've been racking our brains for ways of getting you on board without any contamination. It has not been easy. We actually thought we might have to abandon you at one point.'

'Fire away,' I said. 'Abandon us?'

'Could we risk taking you back to the solar system? Mary has come up with some procedures which we think will get you safely on board without any plant or pollen.'

Mary said, 'Won't be fun!'

'Just tell us,' I said. Contamination had been part of our training. We all knew there were circumstances which might force us to sacrifice crew members. This was certainly one that met those criteria. All of that care we'd taken checking that neither our bugs contaminated Haven nor theirs contaminated us, was as nothing owing to this unforeseen deadly pollen. Tosh's tests were supposed to be fool proof. This aspect to expeditions would have to be more forensically examined when we got back.

'We need to be sure you will not bring any pathogens or the astringent pollen on board.'

'What do you suggest?' asked Tosh. 'I've been thinking on it too. It is like the problem of the fox, the hen, and grain needing to be taken across the river two at a time.'

'Tell me about it when you're safely on board. There are serious hazards involved in what you're going to have to do,' said Mary.

'Okay, it can wait,' said Tosh.

We all realised that Mary was in "serious scientist" mood. You messed with that at your peril.

'We want you to strap yourselves in and open the Rimor to space. Let the entire craft vent into the vacuum of space,' Mary said. 'Check nothing is loose first, of course.'

'And?' asked Tosh.

'We'll then pull up alongside you so that you are adjacent to the other Rimor.'

'Right and then we dock?' I asked.

'No. It then gets *much* more complex,' said Mary

∞∞∞∞∞∞∞∞∞∞∞

Through the cockpit windows, we watched the lopsided bulk of Spirit, still with the spare tank and the other Rimor attached, slowly manoeuvring into position alongside us. Our Rimor was facing to the rear so that the sample lockers were lined up with the matching lockers on the second craft.

We'd already collected all loose items in the ship and stored them in internal cabinets which originally had held equipment we'd used on Haven.

'Preparing to vent,' I said, and hit the override switch which allowed the dorsal airlock door to open without pressure behind it.

We had all strapped into our seats, but certainly felt the initial force of the atmosphere leaving the craft. Now we were living on the air in our backpacks so needed to get busy.

The escaping atmosphere had given us a vector away from Spirit. Using the manoeuvring jets, I returned us the original position.

'Bill, you open the other Rimor's storage lockers,' I instructed. 'Tosh, take responsibility for ensuring all the samples and specimens get transferred. Take a bottle of disinfectant to give a final wipe-down. We don't want any plant or pollen on the outside of the containers transferring with them.'

'Should all be sterilised by the vacuum anyway,' Bill said.

'Not necessarily,' I said. 'Experiments on the ISS showed that bugs can not only live outside the ISS but can also survive the heat of re-entry on the outside of returning spacecraft, so no shortcuts.'

'Didn't know that. Will take extra care,' said Bill.

'The disinfectant will boil instantly in a vacuum, Mark. Don't know how effective it will be,' said Tosh.

'Fair enough. Do your best.'

'I'll be wiping and brushing anyway,' Bill said.

'I'll help,' I said. 'Now, don't forget. Ensure you're tethered before doing anything and keep an eye on each other. No silly mistakes. It's all of our lives at stake here.' An entire crew undertaking an EVA was unheard of. We were improvising safety procedures. Always dangerous.

I saw Tosh take Shooey from his personal locker. He sealed it in a polythene bag and attached it to his suit. I guessed he'd either give it to her family or keep it as a memento for himself. We left our Rimor, tethered ourselves to the exterior fixings, and, one at a time, we transferred to the other Rimor, re-tethering before beginning operations. Working almost at the full extent of his tether, Tosh opened our storage lockers and began handing the sample containers to Bill and me. We all wiped the exteriors of each item and did the same before storing them. Bill was the extra pair of eyes, watching for the telltale signs of the plant or pollen. The whole exercise took close to three hours.

Tosh sealed the lockers on Rimor, leaving the vents open to space. We also left the dorsal airlock ajar. Finally, we were ready to enter Spirit's main airlock. I watched Tosh's final task outside, adding Shooey to an empty specimen locker, before sealing it and making his way to the airlock to join me and Bill.

'That was a nice gesture, keeping the toy. I'd grown attached to Chi. Lovely sense of humour,' said Bill.

'Might give her parents some comfort,' Tosh said, still not giving away that he and Chi had been an item.

Once we were all in the sealed Spirit airlock, we found Anna's detailed handwritten instructions taped to the wall.

First, we had to open a container which released a brownish-yellow coloured poison gas which Mary had concocted. A horrible colour like the twentieth century's peasouper smog filled the airlock.

'Move around in the gas,' said Mary. 'It needs to get into all of the crevices. Flex every suit joint.'

'Five minutes up,' I said.

'Now tether yourselves and hold on tight,' said Mary. 'I'm opening the outer airlock without depressurising. You'll need a seriously secure grip!'

191

Breaking all safety procedures, we heard the airlock door click then it swung violently outwards, pushed by the escaping mixture of air and poison gas. The suction tried to drag us with it.

'That should have done the trick,' said Tosh. If Tosh was happy with the procedures, that meant it'd probably be fine.

'Reseal the airlock,' said Mary. 'Then get out of your suits and all clothes. You'll find an extra powerful disinfectant spray in the green bottle in the medical cabinet.'

'Got it,' I said.

'Thoroughly spray yourselves with the disinfectant. Sorry, but you'll need to spray it into your open eyes and mouths et cetera. It will sting. Don't breathe it in, but empty your lungs thoroughly before you spray your mouth and throat.'

'And don't miss any crevices or body parts!' said Anna with a laugh.

'I think you're enjoying this,' said Bill.

'Even more when you come in,' said Anna. 'I've set up cameras to record our safety procedures as a lesson for future astronauts.'

'You're evil!' said Tosh. 'I will extract revenge one day.'

'Okay, sounds good to us, except the last part,' I said.

We all had coughing fits when we followed Mary's suggestion about emptying our lungs then spraying our mouths. I suspect she knew the stuff would be likely to be breathed in.

'There are water bottles in the cabinet too, for drinking and rinsing your eyes,' said Mary.

'God, my eyes sting,' I said, continuing to cough and splutter before managing to take a long drink of water and pouring some into my eyes.

'What about our Rimor?' Bill asked.

'We leave it in orbit. I'll give the computer instructions to lift it into a stable orbit where it should be safe for a few decades in case we ever come back for it,' said Mary.

'NASA won't like that,' I said.

'Probably not, but it is the only way we can ensure our safety and that of the Earth. They'll understand,' she replied.

'Once we've taken enough pictures of you in your birthday suits,' said Anna, 'remind us to tell you about our little surprise. We've been busy while you've been getting into trouble on Haven.'

'Ah, mysteries?' Bill said.

'Yes. Should help us all lift our spirits a little after losing Chi,' said Mary.

'It will need to be good if it achieves that,' I said. 'I can't believe I lost a crew member. I should have insisted she seal her helmet.'

'That could have condemned us all, Mark,' said Bill.

'How?'

'We might not have realised how dangerous the pollen was and some might have got past our cleaning procedures. It might even have killed us all before we even got to orbit.'

'I suppose,' I said.

Tosh didn't comment.

The inner airlock door opened. Anna and Mary were waiting with more disinfectant spray which they used all over the door fittings and mechanism, Mary slammed it shut the moment we were inside, and hit the emergency vent to shoot our suits and clothing into space, where our old underpants might orbit Haven for decades. Not to mention the extra care we would have to take with our exiting bodily fluids and solids over the next few days. All would have to be ejected via Spirit's dump airlock.

∞∞∞∞∞∞∞∞∞∞

Next, of course, there was the unpleasant task of relating the detail of the events surrounding Chi's death to Anna and Mary which did nothing to raise our morale. Tosh locked himself in his cubicle. The rest of us floated in the communal area, drinking coffee and enjoying the better variety of zero-g foods that Spirit held.

'So,' said Bill, excitedly, trying to lift our mood, 'What's this surprise you have for us?'

'Ah, pretty spectacular really,' said Anna. 'We've been bursting to tell you. Call Tosh.'

Bill went and knocked on the doctor's door and returned. Tosh joined us a few minutes later. 'Sorry. Didn't mean to be antisocial.'

'We've found something orbiting high above Haven,' said Mary.

'How high,' I asked.

'Seven hundred mile orbit. Very stable, between Haven's two radiation belts… or at least where they normally seem to lie.'

'What is it?'

194

'Not natural, that's for sure. It emits a very weak radio transmission pulse about every hour,' said Mary.

'How weak?' I asked.

'Barely detectable.'

'And you're sure it is not a natural object?' Bill asked.

'Certain. We've had long range cameras on it when it has passed close by us, but have been awaiting your return to go and take a look. Ready?' asked Mary.

'Sure thing,' I said.

'Come and strap in,' said Anna and we all pulled ourselves through to Spirit's flight deck, Tosh less enthusiastic than the rest of us. 'We'll match orbits with it as it is due to pass nearby again soon.'

23 Intelligence

Spirit, very slowly, closed in on the alien artefact, and what a strangely familiar object it was.

The main structure was a cylinder, about eight metres long and two in diameter. At the end facing us was clearly a main engine of some description, with a funnel mouth pointing away from it. Obviously some sort of space motor. On the side were some hieroglyphs and two solar panels stuck out, very much as would be used on a Soyuz capsule. We couldn't yet see the front of the cylinder, but it appeared very flat. By that I mean that there was no cockpit area or pointed aerodynamic section. In fact, there were no windows of any description. It looked similar to the Apollo service module, the section used to get the Apollo capsule and lander to and from the moon.

'Can you steer us around to the front, Anna?' Bill asked.

Gradually, Spirit overtook the device and Anna swivelled us around to see the front end more clearly. It was a docking port. Something was intended to be able to dock with it in orbit.

'It's the tail end of a larger craft,' I said. 'The rest of it must have descended to the surface.'

'Or returned to its planet of origin,' said Bill.

'I'm running power scans,' said Mary. 'It's almost dead. Navigation lights are there, but no longer operative. I think the weak radio pulse is all that is left of its ability to transmit. If that's the case, and considering it has solar panels, it has probably been here for a very long time. Look how most of the elements of the solar panels have broken or been misted with micro meteor impacts. This thing is old. Extremely old.'

'Could it have come from Haven?' asked Anna.

'No,' said Tosh, showing a spark of interest in life, 'not once did we see anything on the surface which indicated technology or even sophisticated animals.'

'What about the underwater creatures?' asked Bill. 'Could those things have technology? Is it even possible for an underwater race to build space technology?'

'Can't see how,' said Tosh, impatiently. 'And if they could, you'd at least have expected them to have built exploratory research laboratories and study centres on the land before they started venturing into the vacuum of space, wouldn't you?'

'Yes. I suppose so, but with no limbs, only those shimmering fins, it might be impossible to work on land. In that case they might have gone from the oceans straight into space,' said Bill.

'Poppycock!' said Tosh, always quick to jump on anything he considered to be less than sensible.

'You said you'd been studying planet F?' I asked.

'That's right,' said Mary. 'We suspect it has the same plant. There are seas, but a lot more land. The seas do appear to be black edged, which might indicate the same vegetation. However, there are some interesting features. I'd love to see it at close range.'

'What sort of "interesting features"?' asked Tosh.

'Straight lines. Just visible at maximum magnification when viewed through the Celestron. Particularly one which crosses an isthmus. Could be a canal. In fact, I'd bet my life on it,' said Mary.

'You've not been reading too much Bradbury?' I asked.

'Ah, the Martian canals. Yes,' Mary said, and almost produced a laugh.

'We should really return to Earth,' I said, 'with all that's happened. We can't land on F. I won't authorise a landing with only one tank and one Rimor available.'

'Come on, Mark,' said Tosh. 'We *have* to take a look! We owe it to Chi.'

I looked at him, then at each of the others. Mary nodded. So did Anna and Bill. 'Okay, we'll take a look, but no more. What do we do with this artefact?'

'I don't see how we can examine it. There could be atmosphere inside so we daren't open the hatch,' said Anna.

'Can we attach it to the tank fittings on Rimor and take it back with us?' I asked.

Mary looked serious as she thought it through. 'No reason why not, except that we know nothing about what fuel it carries and spolding could make it explode. That wouldn't be good for it or us.'

'Not being equipped to examine something properly while in orbit is a failing. We must build that possibility into future missions,' I said.

'How about towing it at a distance behind us?' asked Bill.

'No, that wouldn't work,' said Mary. 'It must be attached if it is to join us during spolding. Any flexible link would just snap.'

'Well,' I said. 'We know where it is and could always come back for it. Let's ensure we have high quality video and close-up images.'

The next twenty-four hours saw us record every detail of the alien craft including an alien text panel beside the airlock. Once that was done, we prepared for a spolding jump to Trappist-1F.

∞∞∞∞∞∞∞∞∞∞

I watched Mary setting the spolding target device on planet F. We were all strapped in, the button was hit and we were suddenly frozen in our seats, but this time, only for a second or so. When we came out of hyperspace, or whatever this strange quantum universe should be called, we were in high orbit above a planet which looked remarkably similar to Haven. There was much more snow and both ice caps were extensive; larger than Antarctica. Immediately, we could see that the more sparse seas were all fringed with the same plant we'd found on Haven. It did not look promising for any life on the land, and even less promising for intelligent life.

A klaxon sounded and we all jumped out of our skins.

'WARNING,' said the computer, 'PROXIMITY ALARM!'

'There, look!' said Anna, pointing at a spot on the navigation screen. It was approaching us from the left. Not particularly rapidly, but definitely on a collision course.

'WARNING, PROXIMITY ALARM!' the computer screamed, accompanying it with the klaxon again.

'Computer, mute that damned alarm!' I shouted.

'Alarm muted, Mark,' said the computer, which, thankfully, was incapable of taking offence.

Anna turned Spirit to face the incoming object. I felt thrusters pushing us to port. 'We're clear of danger,' she said.

'Missile?' I asked.

Anna raised her binoculars and studied the space in front of us. 'No,' she said. 'Looks like a telecom satellite.'

'What?' asked Mary.

'Looks for all the world like one of our telecom satellites,' repeated Anna.

Now we were in a slightly higher orbit, it approached us very slowly and we watched as it passed our right-hand side.

Mary studied her navigation screen. 'I'm getting dozens of satellites in orbit, Mark,' she said. 'This *must* be a civilised planet.'

'Taking us down to a closer orbit,' said Anna, applying power. 'Atmosphere non-existent at two hundred miles, so settling for a two-twenty mile orbit.'

The planet began to grow in front of us. Space was crowded here. There were two more proximity alarms before we entered a stable orbit which swung us around the globe, providing us with views of almost everything except the poles.

'Computer,' I said. 'Let us know if there are any launches from the surface.'

'You're thinking of missiles?' asked Tosh.

'Best be safe,' I said. 'Remember, an alien spaceship has just entered into orbit around their world. Imagine the reaction if this were Earth.'

'Yes. See what you mean. What do you think they'll do?' Tosh asked.

We were now in an orbit even closer to the planet than the International Space Station was to Earth. We could see a lot of detail.

'Cities!' exclaimed Anna.

'Yes, and there's that canal again. It is definitely a canal, that's for sure. Also roads, harbours too.'

How exciting. Binoculars were glued to our eyes as we scanned the scene before us. We searched for the same details we'd have been seeing if we were back at home, viewing Earth from this altitude. What luck! Finding a civilisation on our second attempt seemed too good to be true.

'That's odd,' said Tosh, pulling off his earphones. 'I'm not getting any radio or telecommunications from the planet. There are weak signals from some of the orbiting artefacts, but the planet's airwaves are silent.'

'Would you hear them up here?' asked Bill.

'Of course we would!' he snapped. 'Very strange.'

'Maybe they don't use communications in the way we do,' Anna suggested.

Tosh wrinkled his brow. 'Possible, I suppose, but there should still be something. If some of these satellites are transmitting, they must be communicating with them somehow. I've also been sending a variety of radio signals down to them from a simple progression of numbers to some calculations. No response to any of the NASA first principle transmissions.'

'That device which passed by us had an extremely weak power signature,' said Anna. 'Looked to me as if it was almost dead.'

'Right,' said Tosh. 'I'll see if I can find something on a weaker or higher level.' He covered his ears again and began to fiddle with his console.

'We can't land,' I said, finally making up my mind. 'We only have one tank and one Rimor. If anything went wrong, we'd have no way to rescue the landing party. In addition, sending down the tank without any prior communication could be seen as a hostile move. Imagine if something that size suddenly descended into Central Park or Constitution Gardens!'

'You can't be serious!' said Tosh, ripping off his earphones again. 'Mankind's greatest discovery and you don't want to learn more!'

'Calm down, Tosh. I was about to say that we could send one of the rover probes.'

'Useless in this situation,' said Tosh. 'We'd have to adapt it first. We'd need to provide a keyboard and monitor to allow two-way communication.'

'How do we teach them our keyboard layout?' asked Bill.

'Not easy,' Tosh replied, 'but if there is a monitor, we could use it to make ourselves clear. We'd need a sound system too!'

'Could we build the required equipment?' I asked. His anger was even worse than normal. I needed to calm him down. Perhaps a personal chat as soon as the opportunity arose. I realised he was under great personal stress, coping with the loss of Chi.

'Yes, but I'd have to do most of it inside then attach it with a spacewalk. Damn thing won't come through the airlock! How the hell did we miss that potential requirement?' Tosh replied, getting louder with each sentence.

'You have the equipment?' I asked.

'Monitor, yes. Keyboard, yes. I'd have to rig something for sound,' said Tosh, a little more quietly.

'The trouble is,' said Mary, 'that no one expected us to use a probe to visit a planet we'd be able to land upon.'

'No. That's the problem. No one thought! No one ever *thinks*!' said Tosh.

'Getting angry with the entire design team doesn't help, Tosh,' I said. 'You didn't think of it either.'

He didn't answer, pulled on the headphones and closed his eyes to concentrate on anything he might hear.

Our rover probes were similar in design to the Martian Curiosity Rover, but not as large. They were about the size of a Smart car, but had a lower profile, could be steered remotely, and carried a number of cameras. They had low bandwidth monochrome for steering and high definition cameras for taking detailed photographs and video. If Tosh could add a monitor through which this world's residents could see us plus an interface so that they could communicate, it could provide a good method of exploration.

'Okay. Bill, find us a selection of landing sites from which we can make a choice,' I said. 'Mary, you work with Tosh to build the interface. Anna and I will keep a close watch on the surface for signs of life. We should be able to see large cargo ships in the canals and any on the seas from this range.'

24 Probe

The whole exercise would be complex and dangerous.
The two probes we carried were intended to be deployed
in the state in which they were stored. They had an
encapsulating heat shield to protect them during
atmospheric entry. That was to be jettisoned at ten
thousand metres and controllable parachutes would take
over the descent. Once they reached one thousand metres,
the parachutes would detach, rocket motors would fire,
and the remote pilot on Spirit had up to fifteen minutes of
manoeuvrability to find a suitable landing spot. That was
the normal operation. We were now trying to do
something very much more difficult.

Tosh and I were both on tethers outside Spirit. We'd
manually opened one of the RV hatches and carefully
manoeuvred a probe out of its locker. Tosh used various
tools to loosen the cover over the front end of the rover,
while I tried to steady his legs. In freefall, every time you
turned a screwdriver, Newton's third law of motion came
into play. The equal and opposite reaction caused your
entire body to swivel the opposite way.

After forty minutes and much cursing and profanity,
the cover was removed.

There wasn't a huge amount of space under the cover.
Mary and Tosh had taken a small computer monitor, the
size of a tablet, and Bluetooth keyboard, hard wired the
keyboard into a monitor port and taped the two devices
together. They were then forced together, the keyboard
against the screen with a protective cloth between them.
Finally, a strong spring device, manufactured by Bill by
cannibalising a pair of heavy-duty wire cutters, was put

between the screen and keyboard to force them apart when the probe touched down.

The only thing left to do was to push a USB connector into a slot on the probe. Easier said than done. The female end of the connector was not fixed in position, it was on the end of a cable.

'I can't reach in to make the connection, Mark. Can you try?' said Tosh, easing himself away from the probe to create space and accompanying the manoeuvre with a string of interesting profanities.

I peered into the opening. I could see the female USB tucked in behind some other cables. The space was incredibly tight and the full EVA suits had such cumbersome gloves. Holding the cable a few inches from the end, I wiggled the connector towards the slot, but as I pushed, the slot moved backwards in among the other probe cables. After several aborted attempts, I managed to get the plug into the hole, but when I pushed to complete the connection, the cable just buckled and it popped out again.

'How much cable is on the probe end of that socket, Tosh?'

'How am I meant to know?' he snapped back.

'Nothing in the diagram?'

'If there had been, I'd have told you,' he replied.

'Pass me a pair of pliers... and I know you're upset, we all are, but think about your attitude! It's not helping.'

He grunted and slapped them into my hand like a theatre nurse would do with a pair of forceps.

I managed to grip the socket in the pliers and taped the handles shut. This time, when I got the plug into the socket, I was able to push, but it jumped out again as the cable flexed.

'Another pair, please,' I said.

The second pair was delivered with equal medical precision. I gripped the cable, as near the plug as I could and, finally, the plug clicked into the socket.

'Done,' I said.

'Right, let me back in,' Tosh said, taking both sets of pliers from me and securing them inside the tool satchel.

'My pleasure,' I said sarcastically. Tosh huffed something indistinguishable.

'Okay, Mark. Can you now press down on the cover while I cut the tape holding the monitor to the keyboard, so that it will spring open on the surface?' he asked.

I swung around so that I could access the space, held the panel in place, and watched Tosh slit the tape.

'Don't let go,' he said.

Tosh used some duct tape to temporarily secure the cover, then began to screw the panel shut with the monitor assembly inside. The cover would be thrown off when the parachutes were discarded and jet power was applied. That would let the monitor open with the keyboard in front of it. We'd rigidly fixed it to the probe with Super Glue so it should make the journey without too much of a problem.

'Mary,' said Tosh.

'Copy you,' said Mary.

'Do we have to put the probe back into its locker, or can we leave it floating free?'

'Give me a minute,' she said.

Tosh and I both looked down at the planet beneath our feet. We'd completed spacewalks in low-Earth orbit, but this was so different. Yes, there was the blue of the sea and the white of the cloud, but it was missing the greens and other subtle colours we saw on the Earth from this sort of distance.

'I'm worried about this place,' Tosh said. 'Looks as unpleasant as Haven.'

'Not inspiring, no. Perhaps the people will inspire us,' I replied.

'Tosh, you have a go to leave it floating free, but please manually close the probe's storage locker. Did you cut the tape?' said Mary.

'Of course I damn well did!'

'Tosh! Mary's just checking. Ease up,' I said. I could see his face and saw tears in his eyes. Not a good thing in freefall as they stick to the eyeball and sting. 'Come on, let's get back inside.'

∞∞∞∞∞∞∞∞∞∞

In the airlock, we removed our gloves and helmets.

'What's up, doc?' I asked, imitating Streisand's voice from the famous movie of the same name to try to lighten his mood.

I knew he'd either tell me to go to hell or he might open up as he did once in Moonbase about my friend Roy Williams.

He looked at me. He was obviously deciding whether to speak or shrug off the question. 'Chi,' he said.

'Yes, I know. Very sad.'

'More than that for me. We'd built up a real rapport. She really seemed to like me,' said Tosh, wiping his eyes with the back of his hand.

'I know, Tosh, but we all like you. Might get frustrated with your bad temper, but we all like you really,' I said.

'More than that. We spent time together after the Mars expedition.'

'Really? Romantically?' I tried to sound surprised. Had he forgotten he'd told me?

'Yes, she moved in, but we kept it quiet. We particularly stifled it for this trip, but we both thought there might be more when we got home. Now she's lying dead, buried on that horrible planet. Such a waste. I thought I'd finally found *the* one.'

I saw that he was breaking down. Most unTosh-like. I was amazed I hadn't realised his relationship with Chi had become quite so important. He'd really lost the love of his life.

'You two okay in there?' I heard Anna's tinny voice coming from inside my helmet. She was concerned about the time we were taking.

Tosh wiped his eyes and opened the inner airlock. His moment of emotion gone.

∞∞∞∞∞∞∞∞∞∞

'We can't see any sign of movement on the planet,' said Anna.

'Nothing at all?' I asked. 'How can that be?'

'We've had the six-inch Celestron telescope on the job,' said Bill. 'There seem to be boats in harbours and there is even one in Mary's canal, but no movement. No cars moving or anything similar. It's freaky.'

'So, where are we landing?' I asked.

'There's a coastal city here,' said Bill, showing me a photograph. It has some very large areas which might be parks, except that they are brownish rather than green. We're calling it Liverpool because the geography is similar.'

'We thought a park would be a sensible place to land,' said Anna, 'in case there is traffic which, for some reason, we're just not seeing.'

'Can you hit it accurately with the probe, Anna?' I asked.

'I can have a damn good try,' she said.

'Okay. Let's go for it.'

∞∞∞∞∞∞∞∞∞∞∞∞

The five of us sat on our couches on the bridge, strapped in to stop us floating away, watching the large monitor which sat just to the left of Anna's pilot seat.

Anna had a plug-in console in front of her with a joystick and various other controls. The probe was currently incommunicado as the ionisation caused during atmospheric entry superheated the craft.

'Communication re-established,' said Anna.

The monitor was still blank, but suddenly there was a line of bright light running across the middle of the screen and the canopy blew off as the parachutes deployed and the probe swung violently from side to side.

'Chute controls responding,' said Anna, letting us know that she could steer the descending craft.

The view swung to the right and, in the far distance, we could see the coastal city we'd decided was our target.

210

'Liverpool in view,' said Anna.

It really looked like the Merseyside city and had the same large estuary, coastal features and even an alien Birkenhead on the opposite side of the water.

The descent was steady and continued towards the centre of the conurbation. The parklike area grew in size.

'Chutes being discarded in three, two, one,' said Anna, and we saw the probe begin to plummet, then stop in mid-air and continue in the direction of the park, but now under power.

'There's nothing moving,' said Mary.

It was true, the city looked like the empty cities from the coronavirus pandemic back in 2020.

'Looking good, Anna,' said Bill.

'Yes, spot on so far. Height two hundred metres,' she said.

The probe swung through three hundred and sixty degrees as it descended vertically and came to rest. The dust cleared and we had a perfect colour view.

'Keep rotating the camera, Anna,' I said. 'I want to see if anyone comes to visit us. Landing in Central Park might scare a few people away, but on Earth it wouldn't take long for curiosity to overcome the initial fear.'

After thirty minutes there was still no movement.

'Okay, Anna, trundle us over to that path,' I said.

The probe moved smoothly forward and climbed the low edge to what looked like a concrete pathway which crossed the entire park. Still nothing alive.

'The trees are all dead,' said Tosh.

'Or it's winter,' said Bill.

211

'No. There is no tilt to the planet's axis. These are dead. Anna, can you go over to that branch which is lying on the ground?'

'No problem, Tosh,' she said and approached a substantial branch which was lying beneath a large tree. There were several.

'Can you bump it?' asked Tosh.

The probe moved forward, knocked against the branch and backed off.

'It crumbled into dust,' said Bill.

'Yes. Dead. A long time dead, I'd say,' said Tosh.

'Okay,' I said, 'let's get out of the park. Follow the path, Anna.

We watched, intrigued, as the probe made its way at walking speed along the solid pathway. There was no sign of life. The ground was flat and almost featureless; the trees seemed to be dead with branches scattered around them. The only other features were blackish mounds of what looked like the remains of miniature bonfires.

'I think the brown material either side of the path is bare soil,' said Tosh. 'We would expect it to be grass or something similar, but it's been killed and has decomposed.'

'You're probably right,' I agreed.

Finally, we arrived at the entrance to the park. Tall tubular bow top fencing ran off in each direction and we passed between two open, ornate, metalwork gates into the street.

'The whole city's dead,' said Bill.

'Anna,' I said, 'drive over to that mound in the roadway.'

The camera jolted as we dropped off a kerbstone onto the roadway. A few metres in front of us was one of the black mounds we'd noticed in the park.

'Extend the arm, Anna. See what happens when you touch it,' I said.

A metal object extended about a metre from beside the camera. At its end it had a three-fingered hand. Anna gently pushed it into the mound, disturbing the blackened debris. It crumbled into dust.

'There's something white to the right, within it,' said Tosh.

Anna moved the hand towards the object and grasped it, pulling it out of the black material which behaved exactly like ancient cloth, crumbling at the slightest touch.

'Good God,' said Mary. 'It's a bone!'

There was no doubting it. It wasn't a human bone, but it was a bone nonetheless. A bone from an animal, maybe slightly smaller than us. Were we poking about in the remains of a person from the planet F? As the robotic hand turned the bone over, the weight of one end of it caused it to fracture and break in half. The section which hit the road surface crumbled into fragments.

'They're everywhere, look!' said Anna as she did a three-sixty with the camera. The street was covered with the remains of what we now had to assume were animals or people. If the decomposing rags were clothes, then these were certainly the residents of the planet, lying where they'd died, a long, long time in the past.

Anna raised the camera and we had our first close-up look at the buildings. This could have been any big city in any country on Earth. Apartment blocks or office structures lined the streets. They had doorways, a little shorter than we might have, but they were clearly entrances. Upper floors had rows of windows, some still glazed, but many had lost their glass. A few of the buildings were clearly collapsing. Rubble from fallen walls lay in the streets, showing how they'd fallen. Had there been earthquakes? When the probe hit the pavement or sidewalk, we could see shards of glass littering the walkway. How long ago had this plague occurred? It looked like decades or even hundreds of years.

'Where are we in relation to the harbour?' I asked.

'If we head this way another hundred metres and take a left, it will be at the end of the road,' said Anna. 'Do you think that is a vehicle?'

The probe was looking at something which was obviously rusted metal, had glazed panels at one end, two sides and metal wheels. Whatever material had covered the wheels had crumbled away, leaving black flecks of itself surrounding them.

'Yes, I think it is,' said Mary.

'Take care to avoid rubble. We don't want to lose the rover to a fall of masonry,' said Bill.

We saw several other vehicles of different sizes and hundreds of the black mounds of decomposed cloth and bones. At one place the entire road was covered in them and we had no choice but to drive through the debris. Elsewhere, we tried to avoid them, but it was difficult. People seemed to have run into the streets to die. I began to wonder whether they had drowned in their own blood, like Chi. Millions dying when the plant released its pollen. A plague to end all plagues. They probably didn't all get hit at the same time, but the weed eventually got them all. No one had survived.

The probe arrived at the junction. We turned left and the sea was visible in the distance. We trundled onwards and soon encountered what we'd all inwardly feared we would find. The plant from Haven.

It was clearly the same. The black, slimy material lined the harbour walls and, in some places, crept onto the main surfaces. On one side was the remains of a ship. It looked like a cargo vessel, but not a container ship, smaller than that. It had sunk and was now listing to one side, resting on the harbour floor, slowly rusting away. It was covered in the growth, all the way to the first deck and a little beyond.

'Does this mean what I think it does?' I asked, knowing that I didn't need an answer.

'It wiped them out,' said Tosh.

'That probe at Haven,' said Anna. 'I wonder if they carried out expeditions to their neighbouring planet, brought the plant back to F, accidentally or as samples, and then found it impossible to eradicate.'

'I think so,' said Mary. 'And when it released its pollen, it caught them all by surprise, as it did Chi.'

'Head back onto that main street, Anna. See if you can find a building we can enter,' I said.

'What are you thinking?' asked Bill.

'I want to at least find out what they looked like,' I said. 'The doors and vehicles indicate something not unlike our size, but I guess the devil would be in the detail. If we can get inside a building we might find paintings, sculptures, or photographs of them.'

'Good idea,' said Tosh, 'I'd hate to leave this tragic civilisation without putting a face to them.'

'Maybe they escaped to another of the Trappist-1 worlds,' suggested Bill.

'Possible, I suppose,' I acknowledged.

'We need to find out,' Bill said. 'Which other worlds are habitable, Mary?'

'A, B and C are too hot. We thought G might be okay, but while you were on Haven, we studied it. Maximum surface temperature was minus forty centigrade. D is the only possibility, but very small and might also be too hot,' said Mary.

'When we finish here, we'll check D,' I said. 'What are we going to call this world. We can't talk about the people of the planet F. They must have a name.'

'How about Quietus,' said Anna. 'This world has died and will never reawaken.'

We all looked at each other. There were a couple of nods, no one objected. 'Quietus it is,' I said.

We travelled the length of the street from the park and found not one building where the doors would allow us access. Anna charged at one building's entrance, but the central door strut would not break to allow us in. She used the rover's powerful lights to scan the interior walls, but any works of art had long since fallen from their mountings and lay as debris on dust covered floors.

'We need to recharge the batteries,' said Anna. 'They're almost drained. The solar panels are not replacing our usage in this Trappist-1 light. There's a big open square ahead. It should get what sun there is if we park centrally.'

'Sounds like a plan,' said Tosh.

'They'll take a while to recharge,' said Bill. 'Two or three hours this evening and another couple in the morning, at least.'

'We're not in a hurry,' I said.

We turned into the city square and there, almost directly in front of us was a statue. We had our image of the Quietus inhabitants.

'Wow,' said Anna. 'Fascinating.'

The plinth, about four metres by eight was constructed from polished white stone, perhaps a marble, and one side showed some hieroglyphs. Atop it, the sculpture was in jet black. An extraordinary beast filled the space and its limbs overhung the stonework.

At the front, a muscular neck stretched forward with the head turning at an angle to intimidate anyone coming into the square. Its gaze was focused upon us. The body was covered in hair, shaggy hair, as with a lion's mane. One leg pawed the air in front of it while a second supported the weight of its forequarters. Two arms with hands and digits, appeared from the shoulders, one of which was pointing directly at us, as if accusing us of entering the square without permission. It was obviously designed to give just that impression. The sculptor must have been very talented. The animal's back was long and rippled, rising and falling three times before reaching the creature's rear end.

The probe slowly circled the plinth so that we could see the rear quarters. The gluteal muscles were huge and led into four back legs, two on each side. The powerful rear pair provided the support and indicated speed and power. The forward set were smaller, with digits, barely touching the ground. Almost like a second pair of arms. A bushy, flowing tail exited the rear end and the sculptor had caught it swishing as if in full flight. This beast was in mid stride, moving aggressively towards the corner of the square where we had entered. If it had been a real animal, it would certainly have inspired dread.

Upon its back, a creature sat, holding reins that lead to the mouth of the beast, but which had, sadly, decomposed with the passage of time. They now hung groundward, loose fragments of rusted metal.

The rover returned to the front of the statue and Anna tilted the camera and zoomed in on the rider.

He, she, or it was not quite seated, but had risen up. Its feet, not unlike ours, were in stirrups which hung over the animal; a second and third pair of stirrups were in position behind the creature. This beast could easily carry three or even more riders if needs be.

His torso, if he was a he, was short, compared with his legs. He was barrel chested and two pairs of arms emerged from the shoulders and just below. The lower pair were flimsier and it was the left one which held the reins. The closest muscular arm and hand held a shield, pushed towards us at arm's length as if parrying our approach. An ornate pattern or crest adorned the shield. The further muscular arm carried a small bow which was being fed an arrow by the smaller right arm beneath. The head, small in comparison with the torso, looked directly at the corner of the square, following the gaze of the beast he rode.

The face was small, pointed at the front, with a narrow jaw which was slightly open, revealing teeth. He didn't have a muzzle though, like a baboon. It was more that the whole face was elongated forward, as if the nose and mouth, on a flexible face, had been stretched forward. Not flat like ours. There were two eyes, but it was impossible to describe them as the sculptor had just made slits containing eyeballs with tiny holes for pupils. Ears were absent, or they could have been hidden in the mop of feather-like hair which flowed almost to his waist.

'So, this is a Quietusian,' said Anna.

'Looks fierce,' Bill said.

'Yes, but so do many of our statues,' said Tosh. 'They often depict battle scenes.'

'Pictures from all sides, please, Anna,' I said.

219

It was undoubtedly a great work of art and perhaps a fitting way for us to celebrate the one-time existence of a race we might never have the chance to meet.

'I'd better park. Power all gone. We'll get images in the morning,' said Anna.

'Doesn't the probe have a 3D laser scanner?' asked Tosh. 'Seem to remember it in the spec.'

'Yes, you're right,' I said. 'Let's scan it tomorrow. We could then build an exact replica on Earth. Leave it as central as possible to get a full charge,' I said.

'Will do.'

I unstrapped and pushed myself off towards my cabin.

Mary called after me, 'Do you want me to plot a course to D?'

'Yes. Please do,' I said over my shoulder. I didn't want to see any more of Quietus.

I shut myself into my cubicle. It was breaking my heart to think of all those millions or even billions of people that the plant had destroyed with its deadly pollen. I was furious with nature and its selection in favour of the Haven weed. I should have made Chi shut her visor. I was, in part, responsible for her death.

25 D For Delta

We were all in sombre mood when Mary called us all to the bridge. The final data and 3D scan having been uploaded from the probe on F, we were ready to depart, and she had centred Planet D in the spolding device. We now needed to strap ourselves in for the short hyperspace hop to the smallest Trappist-1 world. D had a third the mass of the Earth so a third of the gravity. We'd launch a second probe to the surface if there was any evidence of Quietus habitation. If we could communicate with any refuge the Quietus people had built, we could tell them we'd return in the future to help them.

Spirit emerged from hyperspace and D was floating slightly below and to the left of us.

'Orbit thirty-five thousand miles. No magnetic field, so no radiation bands,' said Tosh, studying his instruments.

'Is that water?' asked Bill.

'Looks like it,' said Mary.

'Take us into a tighter orbit, Anna,' I said.

Spirit gradually spiralled into an orbit two hundred miles above the surface. All of us studied the terrain through binoculars, looking for any sign of Quietus outposts. Had some of their people found a safe haven on this world? Surely it was too cruel to have found another civilisation, only to then discover that a plant had wiped them out. Even worse, their demise had probably happened *because* of their curiosity in visiting a neighbouring planet. Such a cruel universe.

'No radio or other electronic transmissions,' said Tosh.

'Can't find anything in orbit, either,' said Anna. 'If they did come here, they must have gone straight to the surface or they left no part of their spacecraft in orbit.'

'I've set the computer to flag up anything which looks artificial on the surface,' said Mary. 'If there are any bases or structures, geometric shapes or straight lines, it should find them. They'll stand out among the natural features.'

'How long will that take?' I asked.

'Forty or fifty orbits,' said Mary. 'Say three days.'

'Any sign of that plant, Tosh?'

'No, Mark, but water is quite sparse. The ground temperature is between thirty and sixty degrees C. Nothing closer to the equator than the tropics could really survive that. The poles are a possibility, but our orbit doesn't take us over them.'

'I'll give us a polar orbit when Mary's project finishes,' said Anna.

∞∞∞∞∞∞∞∞∞

Apart from looking down and thrilling at the fact that we were observing a new alien world, our stay in D's orbit became tedious, which had the unfortunate side-effect of allowing us to turn our thoughts to the disasters of our expedition to Haven and the dreadful realisation that the same plant had likely caused the devastation on Quietus.

Search as we might, we found no sign of civilisation on planet D. A cloak of depression descended upon us all.

'What about Earth?' asked Bill.

'How do you mean?' I said.

'What will they do with us?'

'Hopefully welcome our return,' I said.

'Come on, Mark,' said Tosh in his belligerent tone of voice. 'You know what he means. They can't allow us back until they are one hundred per cent certain we're not carrying any spores or the plant itself.'

'We've taken great care,' said Anna. 'The samples are all in airtight containers in the external lockers, open to space. As long as the samples are all isolated, we should be okay.'

'Has anyone found anything growing in Spirit?' asked Bill. 'Even a single fleck?'

'No, not so far,' said Tosh, 'but that pollen is almost microscopic. One grain could be enough to begin a colony.'

'At least we've seen how deadly it is. If Chi hadn't died, we could have brought some of it back to Spirit without realising its true threat.' I tried to find a positive note to the loss of Chi.

'I don't think it would have happened that way,' said Tosh.

'Elaborate,' said Mary.

'If Chi's visor had been shut,' said Tosh, 'we'd have all got into the Rimor and removed our suits. In minutes it would have entered the air system and I don't think we'd have even lifted off. We'd all have died in the ship.'

We sat in silence for a while, trying to come to terms with the magnitude of Tosh's horrific scenario. The problem when we returned to Earth would indeed be extremely serious.

'We must make a comprehensive video report of what we've discovered, to give to the authorities and to ensure they don't permit any contamination to enter Earth's atmosphere,' I said.

'We should go into orbit around the moon. Safer,' said Anna.

'I can't target the moon,' said Mary.

'Okay,' I said. 'We target Earth and then use Spirit to take us into a lunar orbit instead of an Earth orbit.'

'That would work,' said Mary.

'I suppose I'm not the only one who has their entity watching out for any sign of a spore in our bodies,' I said.

There was a chorus of, 'Me too.'

'Fine,' said Tosh. 'We're probably clear, so let's prepare the report and get out of this fucking star system. There's nothing for humankind here, except death and heartache.'

Now we all knew about the loss of the love of his life, no one needed to respond. We began work on the report and Mary checked that she could definitely target Earth with the spolding device.

26 Home

This time, before making the hyperjump to the solar system, we all prepared containers of fruit juice, holding straws in the corner of our mouths so that, even if we had no physical motion, we'd still be able to drink. All of us had been somewhat shocked at the effects of being in the dark universe. It looked as if spolding would always have to be done in relatively small stages. If we'd had a method of targeting a world five hundred light years away, we'd have almost certainly died en route. Mary was determined to discover why the time dilation occurred as soon as she got back to her laboratory.

'Three, two, one, go!' said Anna, and we were once again in the dreadful stasis.

I couldn't resist trying out my straw idea immediately and was pleasantly surprised to discover that the orange juice could be sucked without a problem.

A fraction over ninety minutes and our journey ended. The Earth, welcoming us back with its beautiful creams and browns and greens in addition to the familiar blues and white swirls of clouds. A gorgeous world. Our home world.

'One hundred and sixty thousand miles,' said Anna.

'Take us in,' I said. 'Once we've discussed the problem with NASA, we can soon put in a course to the moon for decontamination.'

Imperceptibly slowly, the globe began to fill our view. So lovely, incomparably beautiful compared with the dirty black and brown worlds of Trappist-1. I wondered if Quietus would have looked like Earth if we had arrived prior to their fatal discovery of space flight. Probably not. The dull red light of Trappist-1 meant that green plants would likely be at a disadvantage. I was sure, however, that the world would not have been as dead as it had been when we explored the streets of that devastated alien Liverpool.

'Odd,' said Tosh.

'What?' asked Bill.

'Not picking up GPS transmissions.'

'I'm not getting the ISS beacon, either,' said Anna.

We all turned our attention to the sensors, particularly Tosh's console which was designed to detect transmissions of any type. What could this mean?

'Is there nothing at all, Tosh?' I asked.

'No. Airwaves, or rather, space-waves are dead. Completely dead.'

'Fault with the sensors?' I asked.

'Don't think so,' Tosh said. 'This is worrying.'

'That's daft,' said Bill. 'Must be a console fault.'

'Don't tell me what's daft or not!' retorted Tosh. 'Check it yourself. There's not even radio coming up from the surface.'

By now we were through the Van Allen belts and approaching a three-hundred-mile orbit.

'No satellites,' said Anna.

'None! You sure?' asked Mary.

'Certain,' she replied. 'Orbit established.'

Mary's fingers became a blur above her keyboard. Pages and pages of reference documents flashed across her screen.

'No. It isn't possible,' she said under her breath.

Now was the time to be concerned. If Mary was shocked by something, it was sure to have serious repercussions. I grabbed the high-power binoculars and studied Africa, which was directly in front of us. Not a good continent on which to search for signs of habitation, but our orbit continued north-eastwards, showing us the Sahara, and soon the Nile delta was coming over the horizon. Plenty of forest and lush greenery in the delta and along the Nile, but no sign of Alexandria and, following the Nile southwards, there was no Cairo and the lake at Aswan had vanished. What the hell did it mean? An awful pit opened up in my stomach. It didn't make any sense.

'Come on, Mary. What's happening? The cities have vanished,' I said and floated through to the recreation area, unbolted the Celestron and brought it back onto the bridge.

'Don't know,' said Mary. 'Working on it.'

Within a minute I had the telescope fixed in position and examined the Nile again before it disappeared from our view. 'Nothing. Even the pyramids are gone!'

'How can that be? It's crazy. Pinch me, someone,' said Tosh. 'How can all of the thousands of satellites have vanished? It makes no sense. Mary, what's going on?'

'It is Earth, isn't it?' asked Bill. 'We couldn't have returned to the wrong planet.'

'Don't be bloody stupid man!' said Tosh, becoming agitated. 'Look at it! Of course it's Earth!'

'Look, there's the Dead Sea and Galilee!' said Anna.

'But where's the Suez Canal?' said Bill

I noticed Mary had gone very quiet indeed. 'Mary,' I said. 'What have you found?'

She looked at me like a child who'd been caught with her hand in the candy jar. She'd gone pale. What was wrong with her? She looked at her console again.

Fear rose within me. 'You know, Mary? Don't you? You've figured it out!' I said.

Everyone looked at the astrophysicist. She glanced up from her screen, like someone who had a dreadful life-changing secret which was about to become public knowledge.

'I can guess,' she said extremely nervously.

I'd never seen Mary behave like this. *What had she found?* Four anxious pairs of eyes stared at her, awaiting some sort of explanation.

'Sorry,' she continued, 'but if I'm right, none of us are going to like the answer!'

END

∞ ∞

So ends enhanced humankind's first visit to another star system, but what has Mary discovered in among the schematics on her console? Why is she so nervous about it?

Find out when we join the crew of Spirit to learn the awful truth. Watch out for *THE SPOLDING CONUNDRUM*, coming to a bookshop near you December 2020.

My game, NUTZ, was mentioned in chapter five. Join the free reader club and you'll find a link in my newsletters to the method and rules. It's totally free to members. Information on the reader club appears at the end of the list of my other books.

Tony's Books

Thank you for reading *TRAPPIST-1.* Reviews are very important for authors and I wonder if I could ask you to say a few words on the review page where you bought this book. Every review, even if it is only a few words with a star rating, helps the book move up the rankings.

Currently, I have written nine science fiction stories. *Federation, Federation and Earth* and *Hidden Federation* make up my *Federation Trilogy. Moonscape* is the first in a series about astronaut, Mark Noble. The second book, *Moonstruck*, was launched at the end of January and this story, *Trappist-1*, is the third, released 1st June 2020. My other books are all stand-alone novels.

More detail about each of the books can be found on **Harmsworth.net**. Brief descriptions follow:

THE DOOR: Henry Mackay and his dog regularly walk alongside an ancient convent wall. Today, as he passes the door, he glances at its peeling paint. Moments later he stops dead in his tracks. He returns to the spot, and all he sees is an ivy-covered wall. The door has vanished!

FEDERATION takes close encounters to a whole new level. A galactic empire of a quarter of a million worlds stumbles across the Earth. With elements of a political thriller, there is an intriguing storyline which addresses the environmental and social problems faced by the world today.

FEDERATION is currently in production as an audiobook available from *Audible*.

FEDERATION & EARTH. Book two in the Federation trilogy.

After the dramatic and unexpected turn of events at the end of the first book, Earth is left with several factions trying to resolve the situation. The new president of the USA is trying to secure his hold on power, while a new group who have named themselves FREE AMERICA, is trying to overthrow what it considers an illegitimate regime.

HIDDEN FEDERATION: The conclusion to the Federation trilogy. How will it all end? It will be released on 30th June 2020.

MINDSLIP: Those who have read this book say that it is, by far and away, my best work. For some reason, however, it does not sell well mainly because it is difficult to categorise. It has been described as Wyndhamesque. Is it psychological SF or is it science fiction at all? Whatever the case, if you start it, you won't be able to put it down.

MOONSCAPE: We've known that the moon is dead since Apollo. But what if something lay dormant in the dust, waiting to be found.

MOONSTRUCK: The sequel to *MOONSCAPE* takes us back to the moon where one existential threat is replaced with another.

TRAPPIST-1: A new scientific discovery, spolding, paves the way to interstellar travel. The Trappist-1 star system is the first destination. If you've read this far, you know what happens!

THE VISITOR: Specialist astronaut Evelyn Slater encounters a small, badly damaged, ancient, alien artefact on the first ever space-junk elimination mission. Where was it from? Who sent it?

THE VISITOR is now also an exciting audiobook narrated by Marni Penning.

Non-Fiction by Tony Harmsworth

LOCH NESS, NESSIE & ME: Almost everyone, at some point in their lives, has wondered if there was any truth in the stories of monsters in Loch Ness? *LOCH NESS, NESSIE & ME* answers all the questions you have ever

232

wanted to ask about the loch and its legendary beast.
Packed with illustrations and photographs.

SCOTLAND'S BLOODY HISTORY: Ever been
confused about Scotland's history – all the relationships
between kings and queens, both Scottish and English?
Why all the battles, massacres and disputes?
SCOTLAND'S BLOODY HISTORY simplifies it all.

Free Reader Club

Building a relationship with my readers is the very best thing about being a novelist. In these days of the internet and email, the opportunities to interact with you is unprecedented. I send occasional newsletters which include special offers and information on how the series are developing. You can keep in touch by signing up for my no-spam mailing list.

Sign up at my webpage: **https://harmsworth.net** or on my **TonyHarmsworthAuthor** Facebook page and you will know when my books are released and will get free material from time to time and other information.

If you have questions, don't hesitate to write to me at **Tony@Harmsworth.net**.

My game, NUTZ, was mentioned in chapter five. Join the free reader club and you'll find a link in my newsletters to the method and rules. It's totally free to anyone who has read this book.

Printed in Great Britain
by Amazon